NO

perfect

MAN

An Imperfection Series Novel

D.D. LORENZO

No Perfect Man
An Imperfection Series Novel
Copyright © 2019 by D.D. Lorenzo

Cover design by Judi Perkins of Concierge Literary Designs
https://www.cldesignsky.com

Editing by Connie Miconi, Lucky 13
http://www.lucky13bookreviews.com/

Formally titled *Positive Negativity* (Depth of Emotion series) – 2nd edition
Copyright © 2016-17 by D.D. Lorenzo

Library of Congress Cataloging-in-Publication Data

Lorenzo, D.D.
No Perfect Man (Imperfection Series) – 1st edition
ISBN-13: 978-0-9986 106-3-4

CHAPTER
One

Declan

*G*otta love the view.

I had watched her for days. She was a natural beauty and seemed completely unaware of me. Almost ethereal, she was effervescent, sparkling, and floating in the sunrise scene before me. A woman who was the epitome of my personal definition of beauty. She certainly didn't look like the manufactured images I was used to from Madison Avenue. Walking with an air of innocence, she had me hooked from the first moment I saw her.

As she walked along the shoreline, I simply sat back and enjoyed the show. Nothing more beautiful competed for my attention and nothing rivaled my view of her.

The summer season had come to a close, taking with it the manic pace that accompanied thousands of vacationers. Fall at the beach was such a quiet time of year. I was the beautiful girl's one-man audience. Watching her had quickly become my favorite way to spend the morning.

She always walked at sunrise and I was an early riser. Always had been. It fit well with my lifestyle and maintaining my body as a marketable product. It also meant ungodly hours of working out. I'd been slacking since I was on vacation, but still I woke up before the crack of dawn.

I came here to get away from the city. The New York fashion industry was a demanding mistress and early morning gym time was a necessity for guys like me. We all struggled to fight the effects of time. There wasn't a person I knew in the industry who didn't know the rules of strict diet and exercise. It was a crucial fact of life if we wanted to ensure a steady stream of income. Being a model in a fiercely competitive field, I'd stayed at the top longer than most, maintaining the status of male supermodel. I was lucky enough to be represented through New York's prestigious Bella Matrix agency. Though I was nothing more than a handsome face and tight body to the world, in my eyes I was a bona fide CEO, President, and Chairman of the Board. My company was me: Declan Sinclair. The bricks were stacked with my blood, sweat, and tears, while my spirit was the number one employee. I'd worked damn hard to build it from the ground up and probably sold some of my soul along the way. I'd come to New York with a dream and, in my field, had become the *cream of the crop, top of the heap,* just like the song said—at least for the time being. With washboard abs and a killer smile, I'd been featured in hundreds of magazines and had even seen my face on fifty-foot billboards in the middle of Times Square. I hawked everything and anything that would make a buck. Fragrance, underwear, and fine men's suits had proven to be the most lucrative; I'd made more money in six years than most people see in a lifetime. I was living life on my terms, and now that I could go anywhere, do anything, and buy what I wanted, my choice was to have a place of my own where I could escape. I went where I had my best memories— Ocean City, Maryland. *Home* was a good place. The house had been renovated and decorated in my taste and it was right on the beach. It had been one helluva challenge. The entire structure was saltwater seasoned, frayed, and busted when I found it, but I knew from seeing it over the years that it had two important things going for it: it had endured the test of time and it still had good bones. The realtor told me I was out of my mind for wanting it, but I didn't agree. She didn't think the house was worth the time or effort, not to mention the money it would take to restore it. Secretly, I wondered if some hotel was waiting in the wings to make a nice offer for the property and knock it down. But I persisted because I saw past the old girl's wrinkles and into her soul. She was a true beach beauty. All she needed was someone to take away the dilapidation and give her a facelift. Now, after months of painstaking work and a talented construction crew, she was more than stunning. All she needed was a little love.

The beach was my escape when I needed to get away from the craziness of New York. When I needed some space to think. The atmosphere was conducive for the peace I craved and was the perfect place to hear my own thoughts. The white sandy beach of Maryland's Eastern Shore was the perfect place for me to put down roots; and I was content here. There was absolutely nothing that could compare to an ocean view. Instead of traffic, I heard the peaceful song of seagulls in the morning. The majesty of a coming storm quieted the static in my mind. The massive front porch was my favorite part of the house. Though it had rickety railings and was missing a few boards when I looked at the place, it was what sold me. From the moment I placed my foot on the timber, I got a reaction. The wood moaned beneath my feet and, when I put my hand on the thick post and looked out, I was hypnotized by the panoramic view of water, sky, and sand. Tranquil washes of color assaulted my desensitized perception of beauty and sedated me better than any drug high. I was inspired by those hues and asked that the colors dictate the interior. The relaxed furnishings reflected the real me and the relaxed vibe that I wanted to create. I gave her a name, since most of the buildings in the area had been christened with one. *The Seaductress.* She was all mine. The first place I truly felt at home. On the morning after I finally moved in, I was enjoying the morning breeze and a cup of coffee. No rushing around, no agenda. After living in such a pretentious and fast environment, it was the best feeling I'd ever known.

Until her.

Adjusting for a better view, I switched my cup to the other hand and brushed the sand from my feet as I crossed my legs and rested my ankle on my knee. The stunning dark-haired beauty took delicate steps, leaving indentations behind her in the wet sand. Her gentle strut was prettier than any I'd seen by a runway model during Fashion Week. She was my new addiction.

I sank into one of the house's original oversized Adirondacks. Enjoying the scrape of the rough wood as it scratched my back, I savored my little slice of heaven and stretched out my legs. I didn't know how I would do it, but I wanted to know everything about her. She appeared each morning around the same time, seemingly lost in her own world. She didn't notice me, which was a good thing. I knew what it was like to be stalked. But from the carefree way she walked, I was certain she'd never known the stress of living life under the public's microscope or the prying eyes of the bloodthirsty press. Sometimes I wished that I could go back to that anonymity. Although having the attention of the world was exciting when I was eighteen, it had lost its flavor over the years. Everything I did, no matter how large or small, was subject to public scrutiny. Every day spent in a major city, from the moment I stepped outside or stood in front of a hotel, people who wanted to know me just a little bit more watched me. *The same way I feel about her.*

Ocean City was the perfect place to escape their prying eyes and was the last place the paparazzi would think to look for me. I had left no contact information at the agency when I told them I was going on vacation. *My secret.* There was only one person who knew how or where to reach me, and that was my brother, Carter. He'd found his own piece of heaven in the mountains of Deep Creek Lake. Although our careers took us on different paths, this house meant as much to him as it did to me. It held memories for both of us and that was just one more reason why I had wanted to buy it. When Mom brought us to the beach for vacation after Dad left, things were hard. Mom used up what was left of her savings to bring us on vacation, so there wasn't any money for carnival rides. Carter and I made our own fun. While Mom sat under an umbrella reading her book, we alternated jumping waves and playing Nerf football. Mom always brought us to the same spot on the beach, right in front of this house. At the time, there was an old lady who sat on the porch in a rocking chair. She always smiled and waved. One time we overshot the ball and it landed on her property. We thought for sure we were in trouble because she got up from her chair and went in the house. Neither one of us wanted to tell Mom, but we walked up the beach until we were right at the house. We thought we could sneak up and grab our ball before the old lady came out. Just when Carter stepped onto the porch, the old lady came out the door. We expected to get yelled at, but instead she asked us if we wanted some cookies and held out a plate of chocolate chips. Mom had turned around to see where we were and the lady waved at her. "I want to give the boys cookies. Is that alright?" Mom nodded and watched. We took one in each hand and Carter stuck the football under his arm. Once we thanked her, we went back to the blanket next to Mom. I never forgot her or the house. Back then I had told Carter that when I grew up, I wanted to buy the house from that old lady. Usually, he would punch me in the arm, like older brothers do when their younger brothers say something stupid, or at least mock me and tell me to, "Dream on." That day he didn't. *Little did we know.*

The warm feeling instigated by my memory continued as I observed her steps. She was getting closer and I grew impatient to see her better. As she drew nearer, I saw her in more detail. Long hair, as dark as midnight, nearly kissed her waist. The sun had been playing hide and seek all morning with gray clouds that grew darker by the minute, but it still caressed her shoulders with golden rays. I found myself smiling at the simplicity of her dipping her feet in the frothy edges of the waves as they pulled back from the sand to the sea. The escalating wind whipped the edges of her gauzy shirt. It covered a white camisole, and as it fell from her shoulder, my fingers twitched to return the strap to its rightful place. She was sexier in her innocence than any woman who purposely put on a show.

As she drifted closer, I brought my feet up to rest on the railing and sunk down so she wouldn't notice me for the voyeur I'd become. She was closer than she'd been on any other morning and I was thrilled to finally see her more clearly. Cheeks that were fuller than was acceptable by model standards only made her more beautiful to me. She was stunning in her simplicity and captivating in her oblivion. It was like watching a dream in my head come to life. *Beautiful girl.* The brainwashing of America obviously hadn't tainted her. The photoshopped images in television commercials and magazines had set an unattainable standard for most women. She sat down and wiggled her butt back and forth, getting comfortable in the sand. I leaned forward and traced her curves with my eyes. I craved to touch a woman who was real. I was sick of scrawny women; looking at her made my fingers throb with a desire to feel more flesh than bone. The wind picked up strength and her curls caught against her throat, making my mouth water. She leaned her head back and wiped under her eyes with the back of her hand. *Was she crying?* I didn't have time to expand on the thought, as she stood nearly as fast as she sat down. A rumble of thunder broke through the silence. She grabbed her shoes and a Dunkin' Donuts cup with one hand and wiped her face again with the other. I didn't have time to make myself inconspicuous when she looked right at me. Her eyes locked with mine. *Shit!*

She smiled. My chest squeezed. It happened so fast that I couldn't think. I felt like a googly-eyed high school kid as I returned her sweet expression with a wide grin. As the storm closed in, she ran. My brain registered everything in slow motion like the beginning of the show *Baywatch*, except better. I took in everything about her, including the tiny grains of sand that launched into the atmosphere as she ran toward me.

CHAPTER
Two

Aria

I'd have been blind not to see him. Truth be told, I'd noticed him out of the corner of my eye. One morning while I was walking on the beach, I took a sip of coffee and there he was. It was hard to look away. I kept the cup pressed to my lips so I could continue staring without drawing too much attention to myself. I was stunned. He was so damn gorgeous. I think I scalded my tongue. Thinking back, it's a wonder I was able to swallow. He was better looking than a Greek god. His arms were raised above his head and his jeans hung low on his hips. He was completely stretched out holding onto a beam overhead and my stomach flipped. My reaction to him instantly replaced the numbness that had been suffocating me. I tried to run away from it after the death of my dad and I'd been lost in my grief, oblivious to so much for so long. The sight of this guy jumpstarted my body, reminding me what it was like to feel. Tingles of excitement bounced around my insides like a silver ball in an arcade machine. I missed my dad so much that grieving had become a habit. *But wow! This man!* Just the sight of his slick perspiration-kissed muscles made my pulse race. Whatever he was doing—chin-ups, pull-ups—*whatever*, it drenched my dormant libido with hormonal activity.

I thought he might have noticed me staring, but I wouldn't have been disappointed if he hadn't. That particular day wasn't one of my best. I looked like hell. After tossing and turning all night, I'd debated whether or not to go out that day; but knowing that the fresh air always helped to lift my mood, I went to the ocean's edge. My aunt and uncle had graciously extended an invitation for me to spend some time at their beach house. They sensed that I needed to get away after my father's passing and I happily accepted. I thought that being in a place I loved and experiencing the quiet of the off season would help me to process his death and get back to the business of living. But being alone at *The Skipjack* proved to be both a blessing and a curse. Bittersweet memories followed me through every room. One night I had gotten a drink from the refrigerator. As I leaned against the sink twisting the cap off of the water bottle, an image of my father materialized. He was standing at the stove making spaghetti. He never cooked at home, but vacation brought out his inner Julia Child. He even tried to sound like her, his voice high, shrill, and amusing. He imitated her, relating each step aloud in a singsong manner as he seasoned the ground beef. Everyone laughed at his uncharacteristic display. The memory warmed me as I showered, changed, and snuggled into bed, the recollection fresh in my mind. Thoughts of Daddy engulfed me like a fluffy down comforter. The pleasant feeling was short lived unfortunately, because being near the ocean during a change of seasons meant unstable atmospheric conditions. The sounds could instantly morph dreams into nightmares and just as I slipped into unconsciousness, a squall blew in. It had never bothered me before, probably because I was usually there with so many people. The unfamiliar house noises scared me, keeping me awake until the storm passed and the sounds mellowed. My frayed nerves were nothing more than splinters by then and as soon as the dark night traded its colors toward morning, I threw on some clothes and headed for the ocean. I knew that a nice long walk could shake the apprehension that clung to me like a humid summer afternoon. I craved the restoration I found only when lingering by the sea. The salt air penetrated my uncomfortably tight chest, soothed my tortured soul, and layer by layer, peeled away my grief and pain. The ungodly numbness fell away in the sea breeze and the heaviness that constantly crushed my spirit dissipated under radiant skies.

Although I wanted to remember Daddy and all the good times, when I was at the house, ghosts and loneliness pierced my memories with sorrow. But the ocean air had a way of cleansing me and morning walks became part of my routine.

Today I stopped on the boardwalk to get my usual coffee before making my way down the beach. I was pleasantly surprised to see that the man I'd noticed previously was once again sitting on the porch. After weeks of self-imposed isolation, I was suddenly thirsty for conversation. I had no idea how to approach him though. I wasn't one of those girls who was bold enough to just walk up and say *Hi. I'm Aria.*

Then fate handed me an opportunity by cracking open the sky.

Huge drops littered the beach as I half walked, half ran, toward him. I needed shelter and he was right in front of me. The sky thickened in woolen shades of gray and a chill whipped through the air, turning the sand from friend to foe. A loud rumble of thunder at my back propelled me and I broke into a jog. I was almost there when the clouds split apart and poured sheets of rain. I was the tallest thing on the beach, so when a bolt of lightning threaded in a jagged line through the air, I felt the electricity and nearly jumped into his arms. His muscles flexed under his shirt as I grabbed his arms to keep from slipping. The material stretched tightly across his firm chest. His gaze met mine as he held onto my waist. *Sweet Lord!*

The feel of him rendered me speechless. I could barely put together a coherent string of words. Operating on autopilot, I extended my hand. I didn't even recognize my voice because it had gotten lost in whispered shallow breaths. Looking into his handsome face, the words tumbled naturally from my lips.

"Hi. I'm Aria."

CHAPTER
Three

Declan

Hi. I'm Aria.

Three little words. A minute number of letters. She strung them together and formed a key that opened a world of possibilities.

She blushed and the pink tone caressed her cheeks. The color continued to heighten like the rising sun and when she looked up, her eyes were as blue as the ocean. I was surrounded by people who believed they were the definition of beautiful, but to say that Aria was beautiful would have been an understatement. The twenty-first century modeling industry had corrupted the meaning of the word. Tall? She wasn't at all. Skinny? No way. Exotic? She was none of those things. She was stunning.

Electricity coursed through me. Insanely, my heart raced like a school boy seeing his first crush. My body instantly reacted, almost to the point of embarrassment. Though I'd been photographed with some of the most desirable women in the world, seeing Aria up close ruined my perspective forever. Art and history had it right when the old masters painted nudes. She was petite, about five-foot medium. Everything about her was softly rounded and was perfection to me.

We stared into each other's eyes and I could tell that she felt the connection as well. When she finally broke eye contact, she reached down to brush the sand off of her feet.

"I don't want to get any of this on you." She stood upright and rubbed her hands together to remove the remaining grit. "Once it rains, it sticks like glue." Her voice held a hint of laughter. Her apprehension eased when she looked at me a second time and a lump formed in my throat. Her eyes were the most beautiful I'd ever seen and the corners crinkled under her smile. "Kind of unexpected, huh? One minute the sun is shining, and now this?" She tilted her head toward the downpour.

Shifting from one leg to the other, she nervously tucked a long damp ribbon of hair behind her ear.

"Why don't you sit down?" I pulled one of the chairs toward her. "It might not take too long to pass over." As she sat, she inched to the edge of the seat.

"I hope I'm not imposing."

"Not at all." I swept my hand up and down my clothes to direct her attention. "As you can tell, I'm not exactly dressed to go somewhere."

She smiled up through thick, dark lashes. They contrasted with the shade of her eyes and held me spellbound. As if on cue to her changing mood, they became kaleidoscopic. The hues of blue changed from dark to light. I wanted to stare; but instead I pulled my own chair so that I could sit across from her.

"I've seen you a couple of mornings when I come out here with my coffee. Do you live close by?"

"No, no. I wish. My aunt and uncle own a place up a ways." A tilt of her head directed me to look up the boardwalk. "I've been staying there for a couple of weeks. What about you? Vacation?"

"I am, but this—" I looked at the house—"it's all mine." Her eyes widened in surprise and her forehead wrinkled.

"Lucky you!"

A chuckle escaped my chest at her reaction. "I guess you could say that. I haven't been here very long, though. Just about a month."

"It's beautiful." Her eyes traveled, taking in the structure. "This porch is awesome! I'd kill for a view like this!" She slid back in the chair and looked out at the storm. Her expression softened. "You have to enjoy this—sitting here, I mean. The waves are scary beautiful during a storm." Her voice drifted off as she lost herself for a minute in the view.

"I do, actually." I joined her for a moment to appreciate the view before turning toward her to appreciate the view of her as well. "The view's been especially nice in the past few days." She didn't detect my implication or pretended not to notice. I held out my hand and looked at the cup in hers.

"I can throw that away." She looked at her hand and set the cup on her lap.

"I still have a little bit in here."

"I have a fresh pot in the house. Want some?"

She looked at the rain which was falling in sheets, then turned to me. "It looks like this isn't letting up anytime soon. Sounds good—if it isn't any trouble, I mean."

I walked to the screen door, held it open with my shoulder, and nodded toward the inside. "C'mon in."

She hesitated and dropped her gaze toward her feet. Her shoulders stiffened. "I can wait out here."

Sensing her apprehension, I chuckled. "I'm harmless. I promise."

It took her a moment, but then she looked at me. Amusement danced in her eyes. "Spoken like a true serial killer. I think I'll wait here."

"Your choice, but I do make some killer coffee."

She eyeballed me warily before the corner of her mouth played at a smile.

Damn, she's cute!

Her shoulders relaxed. "My mom always told me never to talk to strangers. I don't even know your name."

"Good advice." I smiled back at her. "I'm Declan."

Slowly she walked toward me, pausing only when we were inches apart.

"Well, *Declan,* I'm trusting you. Your coffee better be worth it."

———————

Her bare feet padded against the hardwood floor in soft whispers. I guided her through the rooms toward the kitchen, and she followed. It suddenly occurred to me that she was my first guest. Her damp hair clung to her cheeks, throat, and neck.

"Can I get you a towel?"

Her eyes widened as her hand flew up against her head. "Oh, wow." Turning her neck and grabbing a handful of hair, her expression was sheepish. "I don't want to bother you." She shrugged. "It'll dry." Gathering all of it to the side, she twisted it into a long rope.

Ignoring her, I reached around the corner to the laundry room and grabbed one that had just come out of the dryer. At that very moment, there was a startling explosion of thunder. Lightening lit up the entire house. Aria nearly jumped into my arms, smacking right into my chest. She was instantly embarrassed, while I felt a rush of excitement. Crimson flooded her cheeks as she pushed away from me.

"I'm so sorry."

"No problem."

A shy smile stole from her lips as she lifted her chin. Her eyes met mine. For a moment, I thought she recognized me and for the first time ever, I hoped that wasn't the case. Although it was probable that she'd flipped through a few magazines, I wanted to get to know her as just me. I turned away to get her attention on something else.

"So, Aria ... believe it or not, you're the first person to see the inside of this house since I remodeled."

Looking around the room she seemed impressed and her eyes lit up with contained excitement. "You did all this? It's really nice."

"I did … or at least I signed the checks. A renovation company did the remodel and I worked with a decorator once the construction was done. It took a while, but I like it."

I handed her an oversized cup and she cradled it with both hands. "I love old houses, especially the ones at the beach."

"I can take you on a tour, if you'd like. You probably saw a little of it when you walked through." I pushed off the doorframe where I had been leaning. "Of course, this is the kitchen." I walked around the room. "I like to cook."

"I can tell. Wolf stove. Commercial size fridge." She took a seat at the table and sipped her drink, then slightly narrowed her eyes. "Are you any good?"

"Maybe you'll have to judge for yourself." My cheeky invitation was unmistakable causing her to smile. "C'mon," I walked through the doorway, "let me show you my office."

Stopping just a few feet away from me, she peeked inside the room. "Oh, this is nice." She walked inside and, once in the center, slowly pivoted as she looked at the details. "It's not too big. Almost the size of a walk-in closet." She leaned against the desk. "I don't think I've seen a floor plan like this around here. Did you add the room or was this little treasure original?"

"Sounds like you're familiar with the architecture. You know something about these houses?" I thought she might have seen a few on a beach house tour. I'd heard there was something like that around the holidays. I watched as she walked toward the window, caressing the millwork that framed it.

"I do." She took in the rest of the room, stopping to inspect whatever interested her. I was content to watch.

She sat in one of the overstuffed leather chairs. Leaning her elbows on her knees, she turned her attention to me. "I'm familiar with this style of house. They aren't too common here anymore. Many of the hotels knocked them down when they bought the properties. It's a shame, really. I guess you have to have an appreciation for them in order to restore them."

"And it sounds like you do."

"I'm a flipper." Her smile widened with the confession. "I buy houses, fix them up, and sell them." Her twinkling eyes met mine. *Flip* is the common term for what I do. Historic homes are my specialty. Beach houses are my passion. As a matter of fact, the house I'm staying in? The one I mentioned? My family has had it for years. They stay in it for a few weeks in the summer, but they also rent it out. Just during the summer though. The layout in the house is very similar to this one. They have a bedroom on the first floor, but not a small pocket room like this." She looked from left to right, perusing the details. "I wonder if this wasn't someone's library. Men at sea were known to love their books."

I was trying to wrap my head around the image of Aria with a tool belt on her tiny waist and a yellow hard hat on her head. "You? You flip houses?" Amazement must have shown on my face. "Really? I mean, you're so petite."

She laughed at my reaction. "You've never seen a woman with a hammer before?"

I realized my comment might have sounded a bit chauvinistic. "Sorry. I didn't mean it like that." Back peddling, I plopped into the chair next to her. "I must sound like an ass. I'm just surprised, but I think it's cool. I've always loved being at the beach and I love the old beach houses. There's something special about them. I was really happy to find one that was still in decent shape."

"Seriously. It's fine." She placed her hand on top of mine. "I'm sure I don't look like the stereotypical construction worker." The shades of blue in her eyes danced with delight. She seemed to enjoy having fun at my expense. "If you want to hear another twist to the story, I used to be a hair stylist."

My wrinkled forehead and raised brows were a dead giveaway of my intrigue. She giggled, continuing, "I loved the work, mainly because I had a specialty. I always loved the creativity of it; cutting … coloring … shaping. Then a friend's mom was diagnosed with cancer. She bought one of those cheap-ass, little wigs from a cata-log." She rolled her eyes. "I guess I don't need to tell you what it looked like when she put it on. It was horrible." Melancholy misted her expression. "There was so much that was terrible going on in her life. I had to at least try to do something."

Her sad tone pinched my heart.

"I spent a few hours, ruined a good pair of shears, and made it look like it was custom-made for her. No one ever knew it was a wig." She shrugged modestly. "That experience gave a whole new dimension to my skills and word of mouth spread. I started getting calls from doctors' offices asking if I could help out their patients. I loved the work, but it paled in comparison to the love I felt for the people I did the work for. It changed them and their families too." Her voice trailed off as her eyes welled with tears. "It was hard to lose them, you know? They weren't clients. They were people I cared about. After a few years, it became almost unbearable. I had to walk away. The sadness was killing me. I felt terrible, almost as if I was deserting them; but at that point my mindset wasn't good. So, I made a change." Her chest heaved under the weight of a sigh.

"From hair to houses? I'd say that was a big change!" I was intrigued by her layers.

"Not really so much. When you're capable of seeing and creating beauty, it doesn't matter which medium you use to express your artistic side." She rolled her eyes. "Thank God I'm self- employed. I've never seen an ad for a job that read *proficiency at making things pretty a must.*" As she changed the topic to a more comfortable one, she shifted in the chair. "My dad was the one who suggested the house flipping. He knew a little bit about a lot of things a jack of all trades. He taught me everything I needed to know about home repairs and renovations. I had just sold my salon, so I used the money to start up a new business. I do a lot of the work myself but I also have guys that work for me."

"You make me feel like a slacker. You're so young and you've owned two businesses?"

"Anyone can start a business." Color crept up her throat and cheeks as she shrugged off the compliment.

My tone grew a bit more serious. "You said your dad *was* a jack of all trades. Does that mean …?"

Her eyes grew dark. "My dad's been gone a little over a month. I came here shortly after I lost him." Tears shrouded her dark blue eyes, revealing the war of emotions she contained. I covered her hand with my own, offering a comforting squeeze.

"I'm really sorry."

"Thank you." Her voice was barely a whisper, but she was one of those people who wore their heart on their sleeve. She fought against a storm of emotions that threatened to unleash.

"I have to go." Pulling her hand from mine, she searched for the door. Although the rain had tapered off from a downpour to a drizzle, I searched for a reason to get her to stay.

"Aria, wait. I didn't mean to upset you." I heard the pleading in my voice.

She stopped, turning toward me. "It was nice meeting you, Declan."

I closed the distance between us and took her hand. "Don't go."

"I'm sorry, but I have to get back." She took her hand away from mine and replaced it with the cup. "Thanks for the coffee—and for letting me come in from the rain."

She walked away, catching me off guard and leaving me to gape at her sudden change in demeanor. "Wait!"

Her hand was on the doorknob, but she stopped long enough for me to come up behind her.

In a desperate attempt, I capitalized on the one thing I knew we had in common. "Can I take you out for coffee sometime?"

Her eyes shifted and she looked at me over her shoulder.

"Please."

I put on the most pitifully playful expression I could muster. "C'mon. It's just coffee."

Her hand relaxed and her eyes softened. "Okay. Coffee."

"When and where? I'll pick you up."

"I'm at *The Skipjack*. On Baltimore Avenue."

Somehow, in a very short time, she had transformed me from confident man to hopeful schoolboy. "When? Tomorrow?"

"Not tomorrow. How about the day after?"

I returned her smile and opened the door. Standing face-to-face for a few moments, her sweet and hopeful expression enveloped and consumed me.

"*Skipjack*. Wednesday. Coffee," I confirmed.

Her chin lowered and she shyly looked up at me, nodding. "See you soon."

CHAPTER
Four

Declan

"Why don't you grab a table?"

I walked toward the counter while Aria searched out our seats. Thankfully it wasn't crowded and she found a private little corner by the window. As I followed her with my eyes, she smiled back at me. I couldn't look away as I ordered.

"Two coffees: one black, one three sugars and extra cream."

Her pleased expression met me as I approached with our order.

"You remembered."

"I did … although I'm not sure I'd classify that as coffee."

A lighthearted giggle escaped her. "You just have to look at it a different way. Coffee's a treat. Kind of like morning dessert."

I found myself captivated by her lips. Watching Aria was something I could get used to. She was refreshing and unpretentious. Struggling to stay focused, my eyes traveled from her mouth to her hands. They weren't at all what I expected. I wouldn't have pictured a girl who wore a tool belt as an accessory to have well-manicured and delicate hands. Every little discovery about Aria only attracted me more. She was exactly as she presented herself: simple, sweet, and thoughtful.

I had been anxious to see her again and had walked to *The Skip-jack* to meet her. Aria was ready to go exactly when she said she would be. To someone else, that detail might not have seemed important, but I was pleasantly surprised. Most of the women I knew preferred to be fashionably late just for the pleasure of making an entrance. We walked down Baltimore Avenue and she chatted about simple things—how beautiful the day was, how the still sky had morphed into a soft breeze, and how she loved the scent of salt air. I hung on every word like a boy with his first crush. Once we stepped onto the boardwalk, she slipped her hand in mine. Almost instantly, I felt a connection. For however brief the moment, she was *mine*. A protective wave coursed through me. The intimate gesture was so genuine. *When was the last time I held a girl's hand?* Most of the women I knew were ready to jump into bed with me by the end of dinner. Aria didn't give me that impression. *I'll take that as a challenge.*

"So, tell me a little about you. I probably gave you more information than you needed to know about me." She lowered the cup and rested it on the table while her finger traced the circular rim. Her big blue eyes were like a drug that coaxed out details that I'd have preferred to keep to myself for a while.

"Well … I'm a model by trade." I stared to catch her reaction. Aria sheepishly looked down at the table and muttered under her breath.

"A model, huh? I should have guessed."

"And why is that?" I laughed.

Her brow furrowed as she quirked her lips. "Because you're entirely too pretty for a man."

"I'll take that as a backhanded compliment." Her expression turned playfully smug and I countered with equal amusement. "Don't judge, beautiful girl. I could say the same about you. You're much too pretty to be driving nails."

"No girl is too pretty to pound wood."

I nearly choked on my coffee.

"Declan! Are you okay?" She jumped up and patted me on the back as laughter strangled me. I coughed and sputtered at the same time.

"What? What's so funny?" She smiled and began laughing to herself, all the while seemingly clueless to the double entendre she'd just delivered.

Finally she sat down and stared at me like I'd lost my mind.

"I'm sorry," I said, composing myself.

"For what? I still don't get what was so funny, but are you okay?"

I nodded, still struggling. Her naïveté quenched my dirty mind. "Did you *really* not hear what you just said?" I narrowed my eyes as I grinned. Her puzzled expression only lasted a minute; then her eyes flew open.

"Oh my God!" Biting the bottom of her lip, she stifled a grin. Her cheeks pinked. "I didn't mean it like that!"

"I gathered that." I gave her a playful wink and leaned back in the chair.

"What I meant was …" Her tongue clicked against the back of her teeth as she rolled her eyes. "Haven't you ever seen the old World War Two posters of Rosie the Riveter? I know she didn't have a hammer; but you get my point, right?"

Her laugh bubbled through me with an effervescence that made me feel lighter than I had in years. The delight in her eyes lifted me from a brooding darkness that had recently clouded my everyday life. Whenever I left the beach and went back to New York, a weight fell on me and anchored me in oppressive thoughts. Since signing with Bella Matrix, I'd grown jaded. My success had come quickly. Among the perks that came along with it were a bevy of false friends and gold-digging women. There were few that I could truly call friends. The atmosphere that put me on a pedestal was the same that muddied my spirit with a thick pretentious tar.

Aria's easy-going and unassuming nature exposed my masculinity. It had been quite some time since I actually *wanted* a woman. I coveted her attention on the most basic level and it made me crave her in other ways. When she spoke, I wanted to feel her lips. When she blushed, I wanted to feel the heat. *Personal and intimate.* Her eyes were a contradiction; they lightened when she was happy, while sad thoughts darkened them. I was drawn by their mystery … and by the woman.

Minutes stretched to hours as we talked. The time spent with him flew by and if I could have, I would have made it stand still. I didn't want this to be the last time I saw him, though his admission made me wonder if it would be. Obviously, his career would take him back to New York. I liked him, or at least I thought I did. It had been a long time since I'd dated, but he seemed to be a nice man—and nice men were too rare a find to carelessly dismiss. I was having fun with him and I didn't want to let that, or him, slip away. Certainly in the fashion industry, beautiful women swam toward him with intent. Their game wasn't catch and release. Snagging a guy like him was their idea of a trophy. *So why was he with me?*

If Declan hadn't told me, I wouldn't have thought he was a model. My preconceived notion of the guys in magazines was that they were either full of themselves or gay. Either way, not men who would be interested in me. I wasn't the type of girl that attracted the ones that everyone wanted. I was more the *best friend* type. My past relationships had been less than fulfilling. By the end of them I was usually wondering what was wrong with me. I had been told I was cute and I definitely had a good business head on my shoulders. I was self-sufficient and I didn't want to be someone's play toy. I wanted someone who would not only love me, but respect me. Someone to make me feel beautiful. There wasn't a glamorous bone about me. Guys wanted perfect blondes with humongous chests. Men weren't interested in girls like me for the long haul and a few had made sure to let me know that I wasn't centerfold material. One even told me that I was lucky he was interested in me. No matter how confident I tried to be, when a guy throws a dig like that, it hurts. I hoped that there were enough threads of confidence left inside of me to prove that my self-image wasn't completely unraveled.

"I feel like I've lost you." He studied my face, then threw a glance out the window.

"Not at all." Pushing away from the table, I lifted my bag from the back of the chair and grabbed my cell. "It's getting late, Declan. I've got to get back." I touched his hand with a feather lightness and the connection made him fold his fingers over mine. His eyes were soft, his expression warm.

"I'm really glad we got together."

A smile played at my lips as he stood. "You don't have to walk me back."

"I know I don't have to. I want to."

He pressed his lips together and I saw that there would be no point in resisting. A resigned swallow tickled the base of my throat. He stretched out his arm, indicating that I should lead the way. Amusement inched into my voice.

"You don't take the word *no* very well, do you? I can tell."

A laugh escaped him as he held the door open for me. I thrilled at the rich sound.

"I'll take that as a compliment."

As we walked back, I lightly pressed the back of my hand against his and he captured it. There was no hesitation at all, like he was waiting for an opportunity and I presented it. I liked how my hand felt in his—small and protected. Instantly my thoughts wandered, wondering what it would be like to feel, every day, like you belonged to someone. Warmth coursed through me and at that moment he squeezed my hand. I knew that Declan might not necessarily fit into the category of men that I was used to and that I needed to give him a chance. I refused to apologize to myself for the way he made me feel, because *God!* I wanted to let myself enjoy this. Given the fact that he was a hot-shot model, I was sure that women were ready, willing, and able when he snapped his fingers. I wasn't one of them and it would probably be over before it started, but I loved how my skin tingled when he was near. The sparks he incited fired up my long-dormant libido. I was already approaching the thin line between anxiety and excitement because he kept looking at me with that killer smile. He was much taller than I, so he measured his steps to keep time with mine. We swayed closer as we walked hand in hand. Warring with myself, his nearness made my body respond in a way that was exciting, but my damn ever-present common sense raised warning signals. I honestly felt a little out of my league. *Am I setting myself up for disaster?*

Once we arrived at *The Skipjack*, he followed closely behind me up the steps and onto the porch. As I placed the key in the door, I felt his body heat. I turned. My intent was to tell him *thank you* and *see you around*. But I couldn't. The wind was all over the place and so was my hair. I was used to it and was about to flip it to the other side with my hand, but he reached up and tucked it behind my ear. His eyes locked with mine as his fingertips lingered. He had the softest, kindest look. A host of brown hues played with the gold flecks in them, and his voice was a rustle above a whisper.

"I have about an hour if you want some company."

All I could muster was a nod.

CHAPTER
Five

Declan

Aria was pensive as we walked through the door and I wondered what had changed. She was so bubbly when we were out, but now she seemed nervous around me. Somehow I had to get that carefree girl back. There was a magnetism between us, of that I was certain. I had realized it that first day at my house and felt it even more today. I needed to ease the tension.

Placing her jacket on the chair back, she cleared her throat. She was rigid. Prim and proper. Her posture stiffened, as well as her tone. She became the consummate hostess. *Oh, this shit's gotta go.*

"So, do you live in Ocean City year-round?"

Pacing my steps slowly, I followed her as she walked into the kitchen.

"No. As I mentioned the other day, New York is my home base. I have an apartment there … but I'd rather be here." I purposely used a suggestive tone. She turned and nearly bumped into me. *Oh yeah. Game on!* The closeness was unnerving to her, but exciting to me. She was as skittish as a kitten and I wanted to play.

She tugged on the handle of the refrigerator door and grabbed two bottles of water. Keeping one, she held the other out to me.

Once I had taken it, she quickly passed by me as she traveled to the living room. Motioning with her eyes to the seat across from her, she settled on the couch. I wanted to be near her and I wasn't a rules kind of guy no matter what kind of hint she was throwing, so I sat down beside her. Backing away because of whatever chaos had entered her pretty little head, I let her set the distance between us so that she would have a little breathing room.

"I don't know what happened from the time we left the coffee shop to here, but you seem nervous."

"I don't know." She shrugged.

"Look, Aria, I don't know what you think about me, but since we started this conversation at the coffee shop, let me just get all the super model bullshit out in the open."

Her eyes widened as if I'd exposed her and she nervously gave me a nod. I felt like I might be on the right track. Sitting back, I took a long drink and crossed my ankle on my knee. I stretched my neck and rolled my head from side to side. I saw in my peripheral vision that I had her attention. "Where to begin? Well, I've been modeling since I got to New York and though I'm not old, I'm considered old in this business. I never planned to get into this kind of work, but I always knew that I wanted to earn a lot of money—because I wanted to make life easier for my mom, and because I was a greedy kid."

She relaxed and smiled, leaning back. She propped her elbow against the top of the sofa while she rested her face against her hand. Her eyes encouraged me to continue.

"A friend mentioned to me that there was an open call and encouraged me to apply. I was working as a barback at the time, so I figured I had nothing to lose. I wasn't the average candidate, meaning that I didn't have that androgynous-waif look that most of the guys had at the time. You know. The ones that looked like starving girls?" She gave me a knowing look and rolled her eyes at the mental image. "As you can see, that isn't me." She grinned and nodded again. "I also had tattoos, much to my mother's despair. That was a definite no-no at the time. I thought for sure they were going to laugh me out of the audition. I had muscles from hauling ice and cases of liquor and my tats weren't something I hid. I went to the corner of the room while they talked, put my shirt back on, and was ready to walk out the door. That was when they told me they had a client who was looking for my body type. Seems the company wanted someone fresh and different—and I was definitely that. The rest, I guess, just happened. I've been doing it ever since."

Aria relaxed, leaning back against the sofa. Her expression held questions and I patiently waited for her to voice them. I took the sweaty water bottle from the table. For a moment it was so quiet that the crackling plastic as I twisted the top off was the only sound in the room. As I turned toward her, I saw a myriad of thoughts in her eyes.

"It must be exciting. The work and, I'm assuming, the women too."

There was a playful, but slightly sinister, tone in her question and I proceeded with caution. I could tell that she was trying to decide whether or not to peg me as a player.

"Truthfully, at first it was exciting. But just like everything else that becomes routine, you get desensitized and bored. I was young. I'd never been out of Baltimore. New York was a big deal. Once people noticed me, I went to parties almost every night. Sometimes they were public relations events for my agency and they always paired me with another model for effect. Everybody partied. It didn't matter what was being served—liquor, drugs, women—whatever it was, there was a helluva lot of it. An endless supply. I'm not going to pretend I was a boy scout or anything, but that shit gets old after a while. It got to a point where sex had no meaning and all I wanted was a good night's sleep in my own bed. I've done pretty much all there is to do, all over the world. I'm a little burned out."

Playfulness danced in her eyes and the corners of her mouth lifted. "So are you saying you've been all over the world in just your underwear?"

The girl definitely had a flirtatious streak to her.

"Both with and without my underwear."

She quirked an eyebrow as she laughed and it gave me an easy feeling. I took another drink, then looked at her. "I am slowing down now. Truth."

Her expression looked a little shocked.

"That's why I'm here. I'm thinking of quitting. Not for lack of job offers, mind you," I quickly interjected. "But I'm getting a little too old for this business."

Her voice raised an octave in disbelief. "Too old?"

"Yep. In the world of fashion, I'm an old fart."

She laughed. "You are not old."

"Seriously, I am. I don't want to get out of the business completely, but I have to find something different. I've been playing with the idea of a satellite agency, if they'd be open to it. I've even thought about doing it here. I mean, where else do you get to sit on your front porch and look at bodies all day? I'm sure I can find some raw talent lying on a beach blanket."

"I agree with you there. Especially in the summer. The beach and boardwalk are filled with them."

"That's why I came home. Before next summer I'd like to figure out some kind of plan. You know, strategize, focus on a direction, and put together a business plan."

She pondered my words. I took a deep breath, shifted to give her my undivided attention, and patted the back of her hand. "Your turn."

She looked up toward the ceiling and then her lids grew heavy and closed. When she opened her eyes, pain shrouded them as they misted over.

"Aria ... Sorry. Did I ...?"

"No, no. You didn't do anything. It's just ..." She shrugged her shoulders. "Can I ask you something?"

I nodded.

"Do you have to go back to New York? I mean, do you live there, too, or just visit? And if you do, do you have to go back soon?"

I didn't want this to be our first and last date and I was afraid that if I pushed too hard to find out exactly what thoughts had just caused her pained reaction, it just might be. So I didn't. I let her lead the conversation, but my interest was piqued.

I gave her a minute to breathe, then took the empty bottle from the death grip she had on it. I leaned into her, forcing her to look into my eyes. As I smiled at her, it enticed her to give me one in return.

"Those are a lot of questions, beautiful girl!" I chuckled at her and she shyly tucked her chin into her chest. Her bottom lip disappeared beneath ivory teeth and she looked up at me with a sheepish smile. Embarrassed, she wrinkled up her nose. *Holy hell! She's cute even when she's trying not to be.*

"Let me see if my old-fart brain can give you the answers in the right order. Yes, I have to go back. No, I don't live there. And yes, I have to go back soon."

"I'm sorry. I'm not usually that nosey. I didn't mean to pry."

Placing my fingers under her chin, I tilted her face up until her eyes met mine. "I'm not offended at all. This—coming home to the beach—has been the best thing that's happened to me all year. Even though I have to go back to work, I now have another reason to look forward to coming home." Her thick lashes fluttered as her cheeks grew pink. "Meeting you was unexpected, Aria, but definitely a pleasure."

Her blush deepened, igniting me. I wanted to kiss her so badly, but I didn't want to scare her away. My chest tightened as her mouth parted. Her tongue slid over her lips as I moved closer. Full, delicious, and moist, they were as wicked as chocolate and as tempting as sin. They baited me. There was one breath between us as I pulled her chin closer and pressed my lips to hers.

She coughed. Panic drowned her desire. Her eyes grew wide. Blinking several times, she cleared her throat. With a nervous energy, she leaned away.

"I could help you, you know. If you'd like. Search for a place— I mean, if you're serious about opening your own business. I have a friend that's a great real estate agent. I even know some very reputable inspectors if you find what you're looking for."

The mental ice water bath she'd just given herself made her jumpy. She was afraid. I didn't know if it was of me or herself, but I tried to salvage the moment. I reached for her hand and she froze. Slowly, I stroked the back of it with my thumb. She was speechless, looking at me like a baby deer on a busy highway. She made no move to pull away, simply allowing me to touch her. I lowered my voice and spoke softly.

"Thank you. I think I'd like that."

She smiled nervously and eased her hand from mine. She was cute, all fidgety and nervous. Taking both of the empty bottles, she stood and wiped the table that was damp from their sweat with one of the paper towels. As she walked into the other room, the scent of her perfume tickled my nose. A mutiny was going on in my mind between caution and lust. I wanted to pull her onto my lap and bury my face in her hair. I didn't want to scare her away, but I wanted more. The near kiss had been nothing more than a tempting appetizer. By the time she returned from the kitchen, she had regained her composure.

"How about a quick tour?"

Not waiting for an answer to the invitation, she took my hand and led me through the house. Stopping in each room, she gave me a history lesson on the architecture and short stories about vacations with her family. We had gone through several of the rooms when she opened the door to a closet filled with graffiti.

Written in different ink colors were scribbles such as *I love Matt, Rich loves Shirl,* and *Debbie + Gary 4ever.* On the opposite wall was *Mike loves Sharon, TLA* in red pen and below it was *Summer of 2000.*

"It's like a family time capsule." Her fingers traced over the letters as she spoke softly. "My Uncle Bill said he found it when he was painting, but couldn't bear to cover it."

I watched as she tenderly caressed a few more names before she closed the door. When she turned around, her expression was melancholy. She tilted her head and shrugged.

"Today, all I can think about are good things." The sentimentality in her voice scraped my heart. "That's the end of the tour. *The Skipjack*'s not a fancy place, but absolutely perfect in my eyes."

As she led me toward the door, I held her hand. The sun had coursed around from the ocean toward the bay in the short time we'd been inside, and the shade on the porch side of the house caused her to shiver. I stepped down, and despite the difference in height, the distance placed us eye to eye. Slipping my arm around her waist, I pulled her close to ward off the chill. She leaned in, touching her forehead to mine.

"Thank you for today. It was nice."

"You're welcome. I had a good time." She smiled at my words and pleasure lit her lips. I pulled her closer. "I think next time dinner would be nicer. I'll call you with the details."

Her brows raised as she smirked. "You seem pretty sure of yourself."

"I am. It wasn't a question, beautiful girl. It was a statement."

A hearty laugh escaped her lips and she threw her head back. Obviously she found my confidence amusing. It was a sexy motion and innocent. The combination of the two sent a blaze of lust through me. Without thought, my fingers threaded through her hair and I captured her lips with a kiss. I wanted her and I wasn't used to waiting. I didn't want to let her go. The kiss lasted just moments, but its effects lingered for both of us. Dazed, she pulled back, breathing hard. Crimson buds of embarrassment rose on her skin, lightly covering the base of her throat. I released her. Giving her a wink, I slowly retreated down the steps.

"Wear something sexy."

CHAPTER
Six

Declan

Leave it to the pretty boy to screw things up. Three weeks had gone by and Aria wanted nothing to do with me. At first I was shocked. Then the shock waned as I grew perplexed. When had I become so overly confident that every woman would give me whatever I wanted? When had I begun to believe that I was entitled? *When did I become an ass?*

For days, she monopolized my thoughts. She made me question myself. Unfortunately, I had no concrete answers as to what went wrong, only speculation. I was sure that part of the problem was my mindset. I didn't think she'd say no to me. *Why? Because women never say no to the great Declan Sinclair. I'm an ass.*

I was all alone in this huge bed. It was too big for one person. I had become obsessed with a woman I wanted in it, but she was ignoring me. *She's done with you. Serves you right, idiot!*

At first I thought there was something wrong with her. Then I realized the problem was me. Foolishly, I believed she would fall all over me once she realized who I was. All the other women did. Although I told myself I wanted anonymity, it was a lie. I liked the attention that came with fame because I never felt the need to impress anyone. Then Aria came along. I wanted her to fall all over me like the others did. I hadn't been turned down by a woman in years and I expected her to be like the rest of them. They all wanted the supermodel. *But not her. How do you like that, hot shot?*

Since our conversation, I'd spent restless nights thinking about what went wrong. She had shut me down. *Me!* But as I replayed the scene over and over, I realized the cockiness of my attitude.

"Hello?"

"Hey."

"Who's this?"

"It's Declan. I wanted to tell you where to meet me for dinner on Friday night."

"Tell me? Meet you? Wow."

"What's wrong with you? You sound like you have an attitude."

"Wrong with me? An attitude? Wow."

"Why do you keep repeating me?"

"Who are you? Are you the same guy I had coffee with, because you sure don't sound like him."

"What are you talking about? I told you I'd let you know the details about dinner. I made reservations. Fresco's. Friday night. Seven o'clock."

"And you just think I'm going to meet you there? Just like that."

"Yes. Why wouldn't you?"

"Why wouldn't I? Really?"

"What the hell, Aria? What's wrong with you? I told you we'd get together for dinner and I made plans. All you have to do is show up."

"What's wrong with me? Really? You know what? I think I'll pass because whoever YOU are, you don't sound anything like the guy from yesterday. He was nice, polite even, and you're ... well, you're pretty much an asshole."

"What the hell?"

"Enjoy your dinner, Declan. I'm sure you and your ego will have a nice time."

She hung up, leaving me in a cloud of confusion. I watched for her the next morning, and the morning after that, and the morning after that. I was looking for a confrontation complete with an explanation. But she never showed, which left me with a lot of time to think and obsess.

As the days passed, each morning's sunrise lost a little luster because there was no Aria. The landscape felt empty without her in it. *I* felt empty and the nights left me tossing and turning in this damn bed and the only person I could picture in it wanted nothing to do with me.

Once I got over myself and stopped feeling like she had passed up a golden opportunity, I realized exactly what the problem was. *Me.* I was wrong. The world I lived in had desensitized me to the rules of common courtesy. If Mom was alive she would have been disappointed in me. My mother taught me the right way to treat a woman and I'd treated Aria like she was lucky to have me. *Stupid move.* Now I had to figure out how to do damage control.

If ever there had been a question in my mind as to what kind of woman Aria was, our disastrous conversation revealed the answer with crystal clarity. Aria was a lady, the kind of woman you wanted to impress. The type you invested your time, your money, and your heart in. Not at all what I was used to. Other women were into casual everything. All I had to do was name the time and place, and they were there. They hung on my every word and did whatever they thought I'd like. That would never be Aria. She had a heart and she wore it on her sleeve. I wanted a relationship like that, but wondered if it would be more trouble than it was worth. I didn't know what I wanted. *What the hell is wrong with me? Stupid question.*

Her.

I rolled over and looked at the alarm clock. It was only five-thirty in the morning. Agitated, I chucked off the covers and got out of bed. The clock blinked angry red numbers that taunted me with the reminder of another sleepless night. In a groggy stupor, I walked into the bathroom. The cold water I splashed on my face did little except flush the sleep from my eyes. As I pulled on a tee shirt and sweats, I followed the aroma of the coffee I'd set on automatic the night before down the stairs and into the kitchen. Another day. Another morning. Another sunrise. And still no Aria. I might as well go back to New York.

I went outside and looked up the beach, but there was no sign of her. Closing my eyes, I laid my head back on the chair and thought of how she'd affected me in the short time I'd gotten to know her. Her smile, her laugh, and her eyes were permanently etched in my mind. She was like a drug that addicted you after one hit, leaving you tortured and craving for more.

One after another, images tumbled through my mind; the one of her at the coffee shop came unbidden. I couldn't resist sinking into the pleasure of remembering her as she shyly tucked her hair behind her ear—the way the curtain of strands caressed her neck as it toyed with the curve of her throat. It played and swished against her collarbone as she talked. I hungered for her unpretentious simplicity. From across the table, her lips had begged to be kissed and her body had filled me with all kinds of illicit thoughts. I had gone to sleep that night thinking of her and had awakened with a hardness that begged for her attention. Every thought of her provided equal opportunity torture to my body and mind. I had to fix this. *Could I fix this?*

I went inside to get another cup of coffee. I had to shake the shit from my brain and figure out how to win her over enough to get another chance. *Just go up to The Skipjack? Knock on the door and tell her I was a jerk?* My pride might take a hit, but Aria would probably appreciate the honesty if I told her the truth. *I'm sorry.* Instead of giving her some bullshit lines to justify my asinine behavior.

My fingers slid on the screen as I pushed open the storm door. I barely noticed the slamming sound behind me as I played several scenarios through my mind. Sunlight flooded the first few inches of the porch floor, leaving it warm beneath my feet. I was climbing over the fat wooden arm of the chair when I saw her. I froze.

CHAPTER
Seven

Declan

My heart jumped from my chest to my throat. She was breathtakingly beautiful. I wanted her. I knew I had to have her; the only thing separating us was a few hundred feet and a misunderstanding. *Go get the girl!*

I didn't know what to say or how it would come across. I'd made plenty of apologies in my messages. But to not take this chance would make me either a stupid prick or a defeated fool. *Go get the girl!*

A thousand tortured thoughts sliced my brain with razor-like precision as I carried my mug with a firm grip and slowly made my way down the beach. My feet moved with mindless steps until I approached her from behind. I didn't want to scare her, but if she was aware of me she gave no indication. My mouth went as dry as cotton, leaving only the tang from salt air lingering on my tongue. I cleared my throat.

"Hi."

She turned. As her chin tilted up, I saw my pathetic reflection mirrored in the lenses of her sunglasses.

"Hi yourself."

Nonchalantly, she returned to her former position. The sun brightened her face, giving her an ethereal glow. My mind wandered at the thought of seeing Aria like this every morning. It would either be the death of me or bring me back to life. I stood awkward and speechless, hypnotized by the beauty of the sunlight playing with flaming tones of red and amber within her dark hair.

"Care if I sit?"

"Suit yourself."

She didn't move, barely acknowledging my presence. Tentatively, I lowered myself to sit beside her, the sand shifting beneath my weight.

"How are you?"

"I'm okay."

Her voice held no hint of arrogance or malice. It was as quiet as a reverent whisper in the midst of a beautiful aquatic chapel. Confession was only fitting.

"I'm sorry." I stared out at the crystal blue ocean along with her.

Seconds that seemed like hours ticked by. Initially she didn't react, then she reached around the back of her neck and gathered the hair that had been pushed there by the breeze.

"Why?"

The words tumbled out before I had a chance to prepare them. "Because my mother raised me better than that and because I'm hoping you'll give me a chance to redeem myself."

A smile teased her lips. I desperately wanted to gauge her mood by her tell-tale eyes, but the glasses denied me any insight.

"Okay."

What? Just like that? I was flabbergasted. *No. No way.* I knew that shock was reflected all over my face. *She's that forgiving?* I needed confirmation. "Really?"

Pushing her sunglasses up onto her head, she turned toward me and gave me an expression so sweet that I felt the warmth down in my gut.

"Maybe one of the first things you should learn about me is that

I don't play games like other girls. I like you and I think you like me. You were arrogant and presuming, and for some reason, you tried to manipulate me. I didn't like it. So why would I do the same thing to you?"

"I ... I mean ... I'm just surprised." I stumbled for words.

"Of course you are. You're used to something else. That's why I'm giving you the benefit of the doubt."

A tiny sand crab scurried by. It was nearly translucent as it frantically dug to hide from a wave. Aria followed its progress with her eyes. She sighed deeply.

"Declan, maybe all that time in New York has made you forget what normal feels like."

"Maybe." I huffed at the statement. She was too close to the truth.

"It's simple really." She turned, capturing my gaze. "If you like somebody, you treat them well. I didn't appreciate your attitude. You said you were sorry. I accept your apology. End of story."

I reached for her hand and threaded my fingers through hers. Aria was proving to be just as beautiful on the inside as she was on the outside. I pressed my lips to the back of her hand. "Thank you."

Smiling, she returned to quiet meditation and I gladly joined her. As the morning waves crashed against the shore, the sea rocked quiet and calm. The day was crisp and it penetrated the air, lulling us into a Zen-like state. I stole a glance at the peaceful shroud covering her face. She bathed in the tranquil scene. I moved closer, snaking my arm around the back of her until my hand found her hip. She rested her head on my shoulder in response.

"I'm curious. Why do you always come here, to this spot? The first morning I saw you, you came right to it, sat down, and drank your coffee. It was the same every morning after that."

She shrugged. "Instinct I think, though I'm not really sure. I've always liked looking at the houses down here. Some of my earliest memories are of walking on the beach with my mom and dad. We would start out early, then stop to get coffee. Even though I was little, I had some too—more cream and sugar than anything else. We would sit by the water before the beach got too crowded. It's a memory that I cherish. My parents made me feel so special with just that one tiny act. When we came here on vacation their focus was different; it was more on me. Mom and Daddy were always so busy when we were at home. For as long as I can remember, he worked two jobs and was always stressed. On vacation, it was different. He relaxed and laughed more and so did my mom." A smile lit her face. "It's funny the memories that pop into your mind, you know? Whenever I think of Ocean City, I immediately think of them, each holding one of my hands and the three of us jumping the waves." She brushed her hands together to remove the sand that stuck to them, then placed them on her knees. "When I got older, my cousins and I would grab our beach chairs in the morning and come down here for most of the day. We slathered on some coconut scented suntan lotion, turned on our radio, and watched the cute boys. We even flirted with some of them. We were expected to stay in this general area in case our parents wanted to find us. Once the sun started to go down, we would take everything back to the house, eat, shower, and dress up so we could go out for the night. We hung out on the boardwalk where the rides are; *Freak Street* we called it, though I don't know why. We'd eat pizza from Tony's and ice cream from Dumser's and flirt with some more boys. We always had the best time."

I could identify, having had a similar experience. "Sounds exactly like my vacations with my mom and brother. I was the flirt. Carter was the serious one. Still is. We both loved the rides though—and the girls. We got on everything! I probably ran into you and didn't know it."

"Probably!" She laughed. "One night, I got so sick from going on the Loop-O-Planes five times in a row with my cousin, Bernadette Ann. She held my hand and helped me walk through my self-inflicted vertigo. All the way down the boardwalk to *The Skipjack*. I nearly threw up the whole way."

"That was you?" I teased, widening my eyes in surprise.

"Yeah, right!" She rolled hers back at me, then grew serious. *"This ..."* she looked to the right, left, and behind. "Ocean City has always been my happy place *and* my sad place. It's just *my* place, you know?"

Gently squeezing my hand, she looked at me through a flutter of lashes and I got a glimpse of her flirty side. "At the moment, it's definitely my happy place."

Her eyes spoke directly to my soul and her words tightened around my heart. It felt like the most natural thing in the world to have Aria by my side. I pressed my lips against her hair, inhaling the scent of lilacs and lemons.

"I envy them."

"Who?"

"Every boy you've ever flirted with."

Her bottom lip jutted out to form a sweet pout, while the display of emotion in her eyes intoxicated me. Desire ruled the moment. I cupped her chin and couldn't tear myself away. The look in those lovely eyes was dangerous. It affected me down to my core and I was quickly learning to read the hidden meanings.

"I think that's the sweetest thing anyone's ever said to me."

My knuckles traced her delicate jawline. "That's a damn shame."

I claimed the kiss I'd craved for days. She was soft and tender. Her honest reactions quenched my thirsty soul. I wanted Aria and she responded with emotion and desire. Still gun-shy from the mistake that nearly ended us before we started, I slid my tongue over her lips, seeking permission. Without reservation, she granted me access and I eagerly claimed her mouth. She responded with a moan that made me nearly lose myself. I felt the tender flesh of her breasts crush against my chest. I wanted that kiss to last forever, but she slowly pulled away. I paused, capturing the sweetness in her expression as she smiled and ran her tongue over her lips, which were now full and swollen.

"Don't," she purred while her smile turned coy.

"Don't what?"

"Don't envy any of the boys I flirted with." Pulling my head down, she whispered in my ear. Her warm breath stoked the fire of passion that I struggled to contain. "You're a much better kisser."

Desire flooded me, but she moved back, placing a modest distance between us. Her eyes lit up as she giggled. The sound penetrated, saturated, and filled my heart.

"What's so funny?"

She snuggled into my chest, hiding her face.

"C'mon, Aria. Let me in on the joke," I laughed.

Her voice trembled with a cross between amusement and embarrassment. "Someone just walked by us and we barely noticed. We probably look like a couple of sex-starved kids."

Wicked thoughts crossed my mind. I gave her a lust filled look, my voice thick with craving.

"What do you mean, *probably*?"

CHAPTER
Eight

Aria

Declan stood and offered his hand to help me up. I brushed the sand from my clothes and once we returned to an upright position, he did the same. He pushed my hair back and over my shoulder as his fingers grazed my chin. "Why don't we go back to the house?"

I nodded. A sexy charisma flowed from him as he smiled and it made me feel beautiful. It seemed natural and I quickly realized why women found him instantly attractive. He simply had to arch an eyebrow and sparklers ignited inside of me. It was both frightening and exciting.

To think that this day almost didn't happen made me sad, because at this moment, he was the same guy who originally attracted me and not the arrogant ass who spoke with me on the phone the day after our coffee date.

When he called, I refused to meet him for dinner, thinking for sure that we were over. Done. He was so cocky that he immediately put me off. But people can change and, apparently, he had. He was used to women who said yes to everything he asked. But the sincerity that I heard in his messages penetrated my anger and I began to

43

doubt that he was the superficial guy that one incident made him out to be. I made the decision that I owed it to myself to see if our attraction could be more; that if I got to know the real Declan, not the one-dimensional man everyone saw in the press, I might be pleasantly surprised. When he approached me on the beach it felt comfortable and right. *And that kiss!*

It was succulent and inviting and had me clenching at my core. The feelings were intense and immediate and I wanted more. If we hadn't stopped when we did …

There was a mental checklist in my head going *ding, ding, ding,* as I discovered for myself why women found him irresistible. His dominating mouth … the way my skin electrified when his stubble abraded it … the tingle in my fingertips as they trailed his thick corded neck muscles until they graduated into his shoulder …

"Make yourself at home."

My eyes widened as my thoughts were interrupted.

The corner of his mouth hooked in a grin and his expression said that he had read my thoughts. "Were you even listening to me?"

"Yes …" I stumbled for words. "Thank you."

"You're cute when you're lying."

"I'm not lying!" I playfully protested. "I said thank you!"

His eyes narrowed until the corners crinkled and his smile widened. "For?" His prying tone was challenging.

"For telling me to make myself at home," I smugly answered. "See? I was listening."

"Uh huh." He gave me a playful look.

"What do you want me to say? I feel comfortable here. Are you satisfied?" I rolled my eyes, but the sultry look he gave me and the memory of his kiss left me wanting more. Nonetheless, I continued playing innocent. "So you say you really like coming home. I'm sure you find it much more exciting when you're away."

"That's where you're wrong." A smug expression appeared on his face. "I love the beach much more than the city. He paused, a serious look washing over his face. "Having you here with me makes me love it even more."

I watched him as he rambled on about the ocean and wondered if he could see the effect he had on me. I'd been told by my mother that I was the most transparent person in the world. A girl who wore her heart on her sleeve. I couldn't hide my emotions to save my life and I suspected that he could read them.

He stopped speaking in mid-sentence and walked toward me. His long stride made the distance between us nearly nonexistent. Slipping his arms around my waist, he looked into my eyes. His gaze was warm as he pulled me into him.

"I like that you're a little preoccupied." His forehead touched mine as he leaned in. Declan's nearness ignited a flame that had grown only slightly dim since we'd come back from the beach and his voice lowered to a seductive growl. "And if you feel the way I do, it started with that kiss."

His tone made me breathless and flooded my veins with desire. He commanded my attention as he wrapped my hair into his fist and tugged gently until my neck arched. His eyes held me captive.

"Kissing you is something I want to do again … and again … and again." He paused between words while placing teasing kisses at my throat and the sensitive spot beneath my ear. There was barely a breath between us as his lips hovered over my aching mouth. I drifted toward him but was held in place by my captive hair. He stared into my eyes. Somehow I had turned into a poor imitation of the girl who began her day thinking that she had the upper hand in this situation. It was the same girl who had decided that she would give the good-looking guy another chance. My carefully measured plan of when and how often I would see him and when we would get together went up in a trail of smoke the moment he touched me. His golden brown eyes locked with mine and I was drawn like a moth to his illuminating sexuality. I didn't care if I went up in flames.

His mouth closed over mine. The want and need I felt emanating from him seeped deep inside of me, turning me into someone other than a carefully guarded, independent woman. I lost all reason and thought under his scrutiny and floated serenely toward his heat. It was more than I expected, but not enough to satisfy me.

"You, beautiful girl ...," my mouth tingled as his delicious rumble vibrated against it, "... are dangerous."

His tongue slipped over my lips and danced with mine in a tormented rhythm. Caution puddled to the floor and evaporated beneath the weight of desire. I was more turned on than I had ever been and didn't want him to stop. As his hands ran slowly up my back, I moaned into his mouth. He moved and his hands dropped to my hips. I shivered with pleasure.

"Declan ..." My voice was a cocktail dusted with desire and caution. He sensed my struggle and pulled back.

His chest rose and fell with controlled breaths as he narrowed his eyes and smiled. His tone, thick with sexual innuendo, fell over my aroused body and drenched me with want. His perfect teeth taunted me with a wicked smile.

"Like I said, beautiful Aria. You. Are. Dangerous."

CHAPTER
Nine

Aria

I stretched across the bed that night, thinking of him. The sheets twisted around my legs. *What was I waiting for?* The days and weeks had flown by and our relationship was growing more natural and comfortable with each one. Much of my free time was already spent at his house; so much so that it had quickly become the norm. One night, he confessed to me that he had never before let a woman into his personal space. The simple admission made me feel cherished and special. I loved every moment with him, even when he was teasing me or getting under my skin, and it had begun to feel unnatural when we weren't together. *How did that happen?*

His house, the one he had so carefully detailed to suit his personal taste, was slowly morphing with subtle details which made me feel more welcome. All of the seaside towns had unique little shops. Browsing in them after lunch or dinner dates had become a favorite pastime. He purchased almost everything that I said I liked, so I had become more conscious about words or phrases that I used carelessly if I was shopping with my friends. The girls and I always commented on things we liked by saying *Oh! I love that!* or *That's so cute!* Declan always took it a step further than admiration and would nod behind my back to a store clerk to wrap up the object of my attention. These items found their way into his house, so it slowly began to hold our combined flavor. Those little things embraced me whenever I was there, whether it was a painting for the living room or a set of colorful Italian canisters for the kitchen. I hadn't noticed how much of me had permeated his home until the night I put the canisters on his countertop. I stood back to admire them while he watched.

"There! Fits perfectly."

He hung back by the doorway and I turned to see if he approved. His tanned, solid arms were crossed at his chest. My eyes drifted from his face down to where his jeans were worn and tight. He was relaxed; one ankle was crossed over the other and his expression was soft. Clouds of contentment drifted in the gold flecks in his eyes, while delight stoked them to a warm and comforting amber.

"Yes, you do."

That was the first night of many that he asked me to move in with him. I was speechless and flattered. Though I didn't take him up on his offer that day, I thought more seriously about it with each successive request. I wanted to be with him, but wasn't ready for that yet. Declan's public life had such enormity that I feared it would dismantle our private one; but to appease him, and satisfy my own desire, I made changes in my life that would help our relationship to grow, as well as my business. I completed all of the open work I had in Baltimore and concentrated on building my business at the beach. It was a risk, but one I was willing to take and it paid off. My best friend, Paige, was a realtor in the area. She explained that lots of people bought properties in and around the beach towns for investment or for their own getaways. Most of them needed renovations and they requested and respected Paige's recommendations for reputable companies. Of course she always recommended mine. I cultivated every lead she gave me and before long I was inundated with work. My skeleton crew grew quickly into an awesome bunch that felt like family. They were good people who loved a hard day's work as much as I did. Though Declan had no knowledge of what type of work product my company produced, he was more than supportive. On the day after I had officially closed my Baltimore office, he surprised me at one of my beach job sites after talking to me on the phone. I hadn't shared the news with him that I wouldn't be commuting back and forth any longer when we spoke, but I planned to tell him that night. I was nearly bursting with anticipation as I took him on a tour through the property. I introduced him to everyone along the way and I could see that he was impressed. His expression warmed me with pride. When we left the job site, I followed him to his house. I showered and we went to dinner. We had just finished our meal and were lingering over drinks.

"I have something to tell you." I nervously balled the corner of the napkin on my lap between my index finger and thumb.

"Oh yeah?" His brows arched, inquisitiveness playing in his quirked smile.

"Uh huh," I nodded. "I'm going to move here."

"Really." He fell softly against the back of the chair as if the shock had knocked him there. "So you're finally going to take me up on my offer?"

"Not quite, but I think you'll like my news. I found a place of my own. It needs a little work, but it's not far from where you live."

The thin veil of pleasure he wore on his face just moments before evaporated from his expression and was replaced by disappointment. He tried to disguise it.

"So what exactly does that mean?"

"It means that I won't be driving back and forth from Baltimore when you're home. It means that we can spend more time together."

He blinked away his misplaced dejection and replaced it with a weak smile. "I'll take what I can get."

I saw the hurt in his eyes no matter how he tried to disguise it. It stabbed my heart, leaving drops of our mutual disappointment bleeding out to stain the mood. I knew what he wanted from me. He'd made no secret of it. But the disappointment was muddled with my lingering insecurity. I wasn't ready. I was afraid. Declan's professional world was so different from mine that I doubted my survival if I had to mingle in it. *Especially with all those gorgeous women!* Things were going so well the way they were. *Why ruin it?* We'd built our own comfortable little bubble in Ocean City and I was terrified that I could and would become invisible to him once I stepped outside of it. *Was I enough for him?*

CHAPTER
Ten

Aria

I had no desire to experience the cattiness of the life he described in New York. Designer anything held no appeal for me. My most expensive bag came from one of the outlet stores in Rehoboth; although looking nice was important to me, I loved a bargain. The women that Declan mingled with dressed in clothes that cost more than my car payment. *What if I embarrassed him?* He was already unhappy. I didn't want my ignorant fashion sense to be one more thing added to the list. I was afraid that my naiveté could be used as ammunition for someone to ridicule him. In Ocean City, he was confident and content; whenever he returned from a business trip, he was sad and hollow. I questioned him about it, but he was so evasive that I didn't push. Instead, I let him gradually fade into the calming clutter of the environment he'd created—the one that brought him such peace. When he was in that mood, we would spend the night under a blanket of silence mindlessly watching a movie. It had become a pattern.

My fingers swirled through his hair in haphazard circles as he rested his head on my lap. I knew it would take a few days for him to unwind before we fell into our normal, comfortable routine. I always wondered what he was thinking when he was like this. Declan read me so well that he sensed it. He apologized for being emotionally distant, assuring me that it was him; that there was nothing wrong with the two of us. I appreciated his assurance and concentrated on that, reminding myself that nothing else mattered. When I went home that night, I left him to fight with himself. I didn't know enough details about his work life to take up the battle with him. I always wondered what it was, specifically, that plagued him about his business. He had thick skin, much thicker than mine, and not much bothered him. *Could I handle whatever it was? For him?*

Over the past few months, I'd spent time mulling over how much personal cost I was willing to invest. Being in a relationship with such a high-profile man would eventually invade my privacy and expose whatever flaws I had to the world. It was a recurring thought each time he went away, especially when he asked me to accompany him. I had refused up to this point, but I knew that I would have to come to terms with my insecurity if I wanted our relationship to grow.

He had just returned from New York again, his usually handsome face heavy with exhaustion. I made a light dinner for us. Declan was quiet throughout our meal and went to take a shower while I cleaned up the kitchen. When nearly an hour had passed, I went to check on him. He was asleep on the bed, so I slipped out quietly. When I returned to his place the next morning, I found him on the porch. Approaching him from behind, I handed him a cup of coffee over his shoulder.

"Thank you."

His gravelly morning voice vibrated a ripple of pleasure throughout my insides as his fingers closed over mine. I kissed the top of his head, lingering for a moment to inhale the fragrance of spice and cloves from his favorite cologne.

"I wish you would have stayed last night. If you had, I'd still be in bed." Suggestiveness raised his eyebrows and decorated his words with intent.

"Then neither of us would have gotten anything done today." Whispering the words against his ear, I took a seat beside him. His weak smile and messy bedhead made my stomach do somersaults.

We sat in silence, enjoying the serene, calming lull of the waves. When his posture suggested that he had decompressed, I pivoted in my seat to face him and sat sideways with my legs crossed in Indian fashion.

"Do you feel better today? I didn't hang around last night because you seemed really tense."

"Much." He squeezed my hand. I read the silent plea before he spoke the words. His eyes looked deeply into mine. "But I'd feel even better if you'd move in."

It wasn't the first time he'd brought the subject up. As he lifted the back of my hand to his lips, he pressed a kiss to it. This was the killer move. The one that made me feel like a princess and nearly melted me into a puddle.

"I'm still thinking about it." Although my voice was soft, my heart beat harder than I could ever remember. I wanted to say yes. *Hell!* I wanted to *shout* yes! I wanted to kick my concerns to the curb and throw caution to the wind. I wanted to make him happy. I wanted to make *me* happy! I wanted to do a whole lot of things I wouldn't normally do when it came to him, but that wasn't my nature. For good or bad, I was the kind of person who thought everything through until the subject was threadbare with scrutiny. However, I was falling deeply in love with him and learning quickly that love doesn't fit in a box. It's more than just a word. It lives and breathes the air of complexity and evolves with time and circumstance. And that's what this was. *Love.* And it was scary.

When I was with him, I couldn't get enough of him and when we were apart, I couldn't wait to see him again. I wanted to be the decisive person I'd always been, and I knew I was acting like a wimp. My heart said *yes*, but my head had a big yellow sign blinking *caution, caution, caution! What was happening to me?*

Change. That's what was happening. Love was changing me.

And I didn't even see it coming. I was a different person than I was when I met him. The woman who was going to kick the supermodel to the curb that day was gone and in her place was someone I didn't recognize. I couldn't have predicted that I would feel this way when we first met. Now I couldn't imagine my life without him. He was right about one thing; waking up beside him was great. There had been a hole in my life and he filled it. We shared everything—likes and dislikes. I craved what he brought to my everyday existence: the joy, the craziness, and the challenges. Our relationship was more than physical and it went beyond sexual chemistry. Our first time was awkward, but he'd been patient and that had made me fall even more recklessly in love with him. I had always focused on using my head and was an expert at getting lost in it, but his lovemaking co-erced my body in a way that made me betray my introspection and abandon rational thought. Something about loving him had changed me, and for better or worse, I liked it. When I wasn't with him, my nights were sleepless from thoughts of him. He was wicked and in-toxicating and I loved how he used his "sexpertise" on me. I loved everything about being with him. I was a smart girl, but he made me feel something I'd never felt before.

Beautiful.

CHAPTER
Eleven

Marisol

Marisol Franzi was considered to be one of the world's most beautiful women. Her photographs graced the covers of practically every fashion magazine. She was consistently in high demand by nearly every major designer. One of the perks of her success was that virtually everyone who was anyone salivated at the chance to be in her circle of friends. What they didn't know was that Marisol didn't have friends; she had pawns.

She had crowned herself the socialite queen of New York. Keeping company with powerful and influential people, she never lacked for invitations to the most exclusive parties and paramount events. The paparazzi loved her and invaded nearly every aspect of her life, which she encouraged. Her ego was voracious and photographers fed it regularly. She kept company with the world's most eligible bachelors. Images of her with them on multi-million-dollar yachts, private islands, and posh villas found permanent residence in the tabloids. Reports of her escapades were chronicled on the nightly news and nearly every tattletale entertainment show. Though she lived an exposed life, she was also somewhat of an enigma. Stories in the press of her background conflicted, and when asked, she chose to laugh off details to create a veil of mystery. Her rules were her own and she lived by them. She did as she wanted, where she wanted, and with whom she wanted, with no accountability. Few refused her because she had a malevolent temper and didn't take "no" for an answer. There was one thing she wanted that had been denied.

Declan Sinclair.

He was her male counterpart in the industry. Their looks complemented one another so well that clients paired them frequently. The visual chemistry of the sultry Latina and the man with the iron stare seduced the public. Nearly every product they endorsed had skyrocketed in sales, so the two were in incessant demand. She was well aware of their striking appearance and how lucrative it was. If she could control Declan as she did every other man, the advantages would be limitless.

Marisol had made no secret that she found Declan desirable and regularly dropped his name as fodder for the tabloids to spin stories about the two of them. Much to her dismay, Declan refused her advances. Instead of discouraging her, the challenge fed her intentions to exploit him. Thoughts of him were distracting and it annoyed her because she rarely gave thought to anything other than herself. He was strong, self-assured, and powerful, not to mention physically pleasing to the eye. She loved powerful men. They were as tasty as fine chocolate and Declan was a delicacy that she wanted to indulge in.

She liked him equally with or without clothes. Modesty had no place in fashion, and though she loved the appreciation she received when she was naked and being prepared for a shoot, lately she'd been agitated when stylists and make-up artists prepped him. She resented that they were allowed to touch him, while he continued to ignore her. Though photographs required poses that suggested they were intimate, when the cameras stopped he refused her lingering touch. She tried to tempt him with promises of the most depraved sexual acts, but her suggestions had no effect on him. It was degrading and incomprehensible—and only made her want him more.

Recently, he had been spending time away from New York.

Having many diversions herself, his absence wouldn't normally have bothered her, but he had also been accepting less work. The rumor going around was that he had plans to gracefully bow out of the spotlight. It was said that he wanted to invest more of his time in the business side of the industry. He'd been trying to keep it quiet, but since it could affect her financially she couldn't afford surprises. They were more marketable together. No matter what he was thinking, she had no intention of losing the spotlight. Lack of visibility was the same as death in their business. Many contracts insisted upon them as a duo. It was inexcusable that he was planning a future without consulting her. She had no intention of slowing down. In her opinion, his aspirations were foolish and her opinion was the only one that mattered. She was certain she could thwart his plans. Every man had a weakness. In order for her to find his, she needed accurate information. Once she discovered it, she would destroy it and divert his attention back to the thing that was most important.

Her.

She had hired a private investigator and was now in possession of the report. She imagined a shallow read and relaxed against the back of her seat. The fine china teapot and a cup of tea sat nearby on the table beside her. She sliced the envelope open. It would be entertaining to familiarize herself with the details of Declan's personal life. The contents included a report and a stack of photos that chronicled his daily activities. She flipped through them and carelessly allowed them to flutter into a disheveled pile on the floor. So far, she was bored.

There was a photo of him having lunch with a man who resembled him. He was handsome, though not as commanding in presence as Declan. She turned the pages until she found a spreadsheet that identified the investigator's findings. The report revealed that the man was Declan's brother, Carter Sinclair. His occupation was listed as Maryland State Trooper. She scrunched her nose in disgust at his menial employment. The next photo featured Declan with a rather plain woman. She was identified as his brother's wife, Lacey. *Lacey? What a distasteful ring the name had.*

She continued on. Image by image, she familiarized herself with his other life and the people in it. There were photos of him visiting a grave identified as his mother's and images of him going to the post office, grocery store, and other places. They numbed her brain. *Didn't he have people for that?*

She kept her interest by acquainting herself with his expressions; ones that he never wore when he was with her. He looked more relaxed than she had ever seen him, even with the pained look he wore at the grave site. It was a Declan she didn't know, but needed to learn. It was imperative that she discover what made him tick in order for her plan to be successful. A picture of a house on the beach, listed as his home, piqued her interest. She hadn't been aware that he had a residence outside of his New York apartment. Attractive, but small, it was much too plain for her taste. The cottage was located in a town called Ocean City on the east coast of Maryland. She viewed photos of him engaged in generic tasks such as arranging furniture, sitting in a chair, and putting up a *Welcome* sign next to the front door, complete with hammer and nails in hand. The only thing that she found significant was an expression foreign to her. *Contentment.*

A whirlwind of emotions began to swirl at her feet and the brilliant red of her Louboutin shoes crept up her body until her temper flamed the same hue. *Contentment? Without me? Unacceptable!*

CHAPTER
Twelve

Marisol

He looked more relaxed than she had ever known him to be and she didn't like it. From New York to a beach? *Could it be this simple? Could a silly preference in location be the issue lending credibility to the rumors?*

Agitation clawed her confidence. Forcing composure, she slowly pushed her stiffened spine into the high-backed chair. She stared blankly as the rumor unfolded into reality. If it was true that he really was retiring, who would replace him? Declan was unique. There wasn't anyone comparable in the market that was palatable to her. She would refuse to be photographed with anyone who didn't meet her approval. The only obstacle was that the agency made the final decisions. Her opinion with clients carried very little weight when it came to closed-door negotiations unless she was on her knees. She refused to go back to sucking their inflated egos to get what she wanted. It had taken her too long to get to where she was and Declan was a huge part of *their* package. Without him, she could be forced to work with anyone they chose! *Unacceptable! No, no, no!*

She threw the stapled papers across the room where they bounced off the corner of the bookcase. Indignation bubbled inside of her like a witch's brew and Declan's inconsideration was the main ingredient. He hadn't given a thought about her! *Selfish bastard!*

She shot out of the chair. Smoldering footsteps carried her across the room to retrieve her cell phone. In disgust, she discarded the inflammatory photos with a flick of her wrist. She was about to punch the numbers on the keypad when one errant visual strayed from the pile and glided toward her. A breath strangled her throat as she looked down at the image. Staring up at her was a woman with the bluest eyes she'd ever seen.

Her mouth tensed into a tight, thin line. She clenched her teeth until her jaw pained from the assault. Slowly she reached for the photo, her arm and fingertips moving like a serpent about to strike its prey. She lifted it, touching only the corner, as if it were poisonous venom. *Who the hell is this?*

There was more than one photo of the woman; a set, in fact, but the first one caught her eye. It was a close-up of the woman's face. She looked out at something unknown. Her expression was wistful. Dark brown hair framed her face. She looked soft, perhaps even kind. All the things that Marisol was not.

She forced herself to look through the remaining images. What she saw, she hated. Declan's expression in them made her particularly mercurial. Image after image pushed the seed of bitterness further down until it took root deep within her belly. The expressions he shared with this woman and the realization that he was enjoying himself made her livid. She dialed the phone.

"What is her name?" her thick Columbian accent accused him in greeting.

Instantly recognizing her voice, he paced his response with a condescending and lazy tone. "Who you talking about?"

"Don't be impudent!" Marisol hated that the man's diction floated more loosely than the tea in her cup. She would never understand Americans. She took pride in her command of the English language, while they took pleasure in the massacre of it. "The woman, you fool! The one with the blue eyes."

He spoke slowly and calmly, as if retreating from a rabid dog, "Calm down. I'm confirming who she is as we speak."

"Confirming her? You don't know who she is? What am I paying you for?"

"Look, lady. You insisted you wanted the information today. The report wasn't complete. I gave you what I had."

"*Que la vaca estupida!*" her voice boomed into the telephone. "I want details and I want them NOW!" She threw the phone against the wall, leaving a chip in the drywall. *Incompetence!* Her instructions had been clear. All he had to do was get information on every aspect of Declan's personal life. The house, the beach town, and most importantly, this woman, were factors in her plan to manipulate him. How could she effectively do that without accurate information?

Her thoughts scattered as she paced the floor. She needed information on this *puta:* who she was, what she did, and how she fit into the puzzle of the life Declan hid from her. The woman was pretty, in a plain kind of way, but Declan was one of the most attractive men in the world. He had to be keeping her a secret because he wouldn't be seen with some fat, ugly whore in public. Her hair was disheveled in every photo. It didn't look like she had seen the inside of a salon for years. She was short. Her face was round. Her clothes were a product of some white-trash chain store and she wore those rubber things on her feet. *Flip-flops!* And her ass was fat. *What was wrong with him?*

Taking a deep breath, she temporarily reigned in her anger. There was nothing to worry about. Not one thing. Of course Declan would come running back to her and his life in New York once he'd had his fill of the fat girl. As far as looks and taste were concerned, Marisol was clearly the better choice. They weren't even in the same category! She placed the photos back onto the table and took a seat on the sofa. Reaching down, she removed her stiletto heels and placed them to the side. Back and forth, she repetitively massaged the soles of her feet against the carpet. She couldn't get one of the photos out of her mind. It was the one of the two of them sitting face-to-face in the sand. The look in Declan's eyes was most interesting. She knew it well. She'd seen that look directed at her in the eyes of every man she had ever known. *Desire.* He wanted the woman! *Damn him!*

Her composure once again began to unravel as evil thoughts unfolded. A sarcastic grin marred her perfectly lined lips. *She's a whore! That must be it! A stupid little whore with a talented mouth!*

A malignant hostility wrapped around her like a fur coat. The woman in the photo was no longer of concern. She was an insignificant, inadequate representation of the female form. *But Declan!* He would pay for his crimes. The average eye might see a photograph as a representation of a person, place, or thing, but she was well acquainted with the camera. It told a story. His smile was loving. His eyes were kind. His fingers rested tenderly over the woman's; Declan was guilty of sharing with someone else what he'd never offered her. *Sincerity.*

Marisol's grip tightened. The stabbing sharp edges of her freshly manicured fingernails pierced through the photo. She had flaunted herself at him while he had acted disinterested. Secretly she had thought he might be a homosexual, and while that assumption posed a challenge, she never believed he was off limits. She was more than capable of stiffening even the limpest resistance. But the realization of truth was souring in her stomach and taking root inside the darkness of her shallow soul. Declan Sinclair wasn't gay! He simply didn't want her!

With a pitch that would have made a ball player proud, the Murano glass whooshed through the air. The shards equaled her shattering scream. Her chest rose and fell with stormy breaths. This would not be allowed! She refused to be humiliated by him and some two-bit beach bimbo! *How dare he!* He thought he could write himself a little love story? Well, guess what? She was the new ghostwriter and the plot would definitely thicken. *Love story, in-*

deed! Before she was through, she'd make both of them realize that *this* story would NOT have a happy ending!

CHAPTER
Thirteen

Declan

"**B**abe? Are you here?"
I called out into the living room, hoping that Aria was here. I'd only been gone for a few days, but it felt so good to be back home again. *With her.*

Aria was sexually naive, but what fun it was to introduce her to new things. She was sweetly modest, but that timidity quickly faded away as I led her to discover her hidden desires. Just the memory made me want her.

"You're beautiful. Your breasts ... I love the fullness."

"Stop. You're surrounded by beautiful women all the time."

I didn't like the tone she used when she spoke about herself. I captured her chin in my fingers, my eyes locking with hers. "I've never met anyone more beautiful than you. Inside and out." A blush rushed up her skin, warming the breast that filled my hand.

"I'm not good at this."

"You don't have to be. I am."

I disregarded her self-consciousness and kissed every inch of her, making my way down her body with eager lips. When I reached her most sensitive area, I kissed her and ran my tongue through her fold. I smiled when she shivered.

"You don't have to do that."

I lifted my chin. I had no idea what she thought of sex, but I was only focusing on pleasure. She was uneasy, somehow thinking that I was doing her a favor.

"I know I don't. I want to. All I want you to do is feel. Can you do that for me?"

Apprehension clouded her expression; but then, little by little, I felt her muscles loosen.

"I'll try."

Her tension slowly trickled away beneath my care. I ran my hands over her arms, legs, breasts, and stomach, teasing ... arousing ... stirring her hidden desires. A quiet moan escaped her lips as the pseudo-massage freed her mind. Satisfied with my efforts, I continued to savor the taste of her ... in many ways.

The memory flooded me with pleasure, making me hopeful that I'd find her here. Kicking off my shoes, I relished the feel of the cool hardwood beneath my feet. The tiny grits of sand, remnants of life at the beach and nearly impossible to remove, dug into my soles as I walked up the steps. I searched through each room hoping to find her. She had commandeered one of the bedrooms in the back of the house. It held several sketch books and a miscellaneous collection of her tools. A desk took center stage among her things. It was a discovery I'd made while driving on Route 50. I saw it in the window of an antique shop and knew she would love it. I brought it home, struggling to fit it in the car and carry it up the steps. I had also purchased a big, comfy chair that she had admired while we were walking in town. I knew that these little things would make her happy. It was an underhanded tactic, but anything I could do to make her feel like she belonged here, with me, was fair game. The past few times I'd returned from business, I found her in there, beautifully immersed in deep thought while sitting quietly. I peeked over her shoulder many times, amazed at how easily she transformed her doodles into visions. I was happy sharing more of her world.

As a player, it was crazy to me how I missed her. Equally crazy was what I was discovering about New York. It was as if someone had given me a fresh pair of glasses. I was ashamed of how shallow and self-indulgent I'd become. Since I had made the decision to move more into the business side of modeling, I'd been removing myself from the social circles I used to frequent. Another revelation was who my true friends were. Unfortunately, I had few of the *true* and too many of the superficial. The environment I'd immersed myself in had made me calloused and jaded. *How did I let it get this way?*

My newfound clarity only confirmed my decision to make the industry a more pleasant place for new talent to work in. I didn't want them to fall into the traps I had because there were more opportunists in my life than I cared to admit.

When I first arrived in New York, I was convinced that I would never leave. Now I dreaded going into the city. Aria was the reason. I felt a void when I left her. She made me feel *real* again. She was the most honest person I knew, but damn, she was hard to impress. Although she respected my work ethic, she looked beneath the surface of the man on the pages. With her, my life was becoming less complicated. Easy. She reminded me to return to the man I was inside. That *who* I was wasn't always *what* I was. The ability to be photogenic was a tool of my craft, much like a hammer was for hers. She helped me to gain a new perspective. The agency kept me busy with work as I honored the remainder of my contracts; but the moment I finished, I rushed to get home. Thoughts of her preoccupied me. While the others went out to party, all I could think of was having a coffee date at my kitchen table.

"I'm in here."

Her voice trailed from the kitchen and like a charmed snake, I followed the sound. I stopped in the doorway, savoring the view of the sexiest thing I'd seen all week—Aria in cut-off jeans and a tank top. My eyes traveled down her back. Her long dark hair had been loosely pulled into a ponytail. I took in the scene, enjoying the landscape that started at the middle of her back and traveled all the way down the back of her legs. Frayed strands of denim kissed them. If she turned she would have caught me staring. Concentrating on the task at hand, she continued jockeying between the counter and the refrigerator.

"Food's ready. I thought you might be hungry. I made sandwiches."

The comments were quick and clipped. Nothing was on her mind but making food; it was the last thing on mine. I came up behind her, wrapping my arms around her waist. My fingers grazed her bare belly and I fanned them over her midsection. I held her tight and she instantly melted against my chest. I tickled the shell of her ear with my lips.

"I *am* hungry." Her breath quickened as desire colored my words in shades of sex and lust. I wanted more than food. I wanted her.

I pressed into her tempting backside. She was now captive, pinned between the granite surface and my rapidly hardening appetite. Her head fell to the side as my lips found the curve at the base of her neck. I drove my hips hard into her curvaceous bottom, preventing her escape. She deserved a taste of what she did to me. Her words rode the current of fragile wisps of air.

"Here. Take a bite."

The quiver in her voice made me rock hard. Her hand trembled as she held a partially sliced tomato near her shoulder.

"I remembered how much you like these."

She turned her head slightly, giving me a sultry look over her shoulder. She carefully manipulated her delicate hand beneath the fruit until it rested on the very tips of her fingers. A haphazard trail of succulent juice turned food into foreplay as it made its way down her arm. I licked it, following it with my tongue from elbow to hand. She jumped when I nipped the tender flesh on her wrist. "Mmmm.

What a good girl. You remembered."

"Yes ..."

Her voice was a whisper. She shifted from one foot to the other to ease her growing need. The friction excited me, making me even more painfully aware of the strained tension against my zipper. It grew unbearable with each second. My appetite for food was gone. The absence of her these past few days had made me insane. The only thing that could satisfy me was to be buried deep inside her.

"I've missed you, Bear."

Her raspy tone played with my mind and stroked my passion-drenched ego. She steadied herself against the makeshift barrier and placed her palms at the edge of the counter. She pushed against my crotch and teased me as she rocked her backside. I groaned. For a girl that, only months ago, shied away from sex, she had become a quick study.

My hands went from her waist to her breasts and I squeezed their pleasurable fullness. She closed her eyes as her head fell back and sensual pleasure veiled her face. I addictively ingested her moan like the drug it had become to me. One hit and the whole world melted away.

"You missed me?" She answered by pressing harder against me and I felt the teeth of my zipper imprint on my skin. "I missed you too, beautiful girl."

My voice was like jagged gravel as it revealed my agony. Aria did a seductive pirouette in my arms, her firm breasts leaving a burning trail on me even with the lightest touch. Only the thin cotton of her shirt separated our skin. I loved everything about what I saw on her face. She looked up at me through thick, dark lashes. Desire filled her eyes. Her teeth sunk into her plump bottom lip. I knew the expression well. She had missed me just as much as I had missed her. The void had made both of us raw with need. Seducing her had become my greatest pleasure. Transforming her from woman to temptress was as powerful a feeling as I'd ever had. I couldn't get enough of it. It released the animal inside of me. I needed to consume her by burying myself in her heat.

Capturing her small wrist, I pressed my lips against it. Her pulse raced beneath. Her nipples pebbled against the thin cotton. They begged for my attention. Her inhibition completely collapsed under my fingertips. I teased and tortured, licking the lobe beneath her ear while nipping at the tender skin. I couldn't stop myself. I tasted and savored wherever passion compelled me to go. Her response mirrored mine as my mind thundered for release. Every cell in my body roared the same message in my brain. *Aria was mine.*

CHAPTER
Fourteen

Aria

*P*ress.
    Release.
    Press.
Release.
Press ...

My skin sizzled under the delicious burn of Declan's mouth. He claimed me with each kiss, inch by inch. Desire made my blood flow in waves that grew in intensity and crashed in silent thunder at my core. My resistance weakened as his touch heightened my senses. He wanted me. With him. *Living* with him—and what was left of the inner battle with my independent spirit was now dissipating as every nerve fell under his command. Because I knew that he wanted me, every experience like this was hot *and* sweet.

We were opposite in many ways and sex was one of them. My naiveté was balanced by his expertise. But he was rapidly teaching my body to respond to him. Every nerve was under his command as I fell free of conscious thought. Caught in a sensuous undertow, I was burned rather than quenched. All that mattered was the hot brand of his touch. I tried to shift my hips to ease my growing ache. I was dying for release, but he chose instead to build a fire. His warm breath skated the surface of my sensitive skin and sent me spiraling with want. His teeth carefully abraded my tender areas and I moaned at the friction, which elicited a low and satisfied growl from deep within his chest. As he nipped, kissed, and played, I barely breathed. The combination of his talents … the way he drove me out of my mind … made me feel wicked. I blushed at the thought of the things I wanted him to do to me.

"You are the sweetest thing I've ever tasted."

Seduction drenched his gravelly tone, dripping from the torturous tongue that fed fire into my blood. My skin warmed beneath his compliment. His hips bore into me with unrelenting pressure, while his hands explored beneath my shirt. His touch cut into my raw need, making me bleed with lust. My emotions were a conundrum. No one had ever made me feel the way that Declan did. My mind struggled to make sense where there was none. Nothing about sex with him was rational. I was a flaming inferno dancing in a sea of want. All I could do was spin recklessly as I burned. He expertly played my body like some mythological god, tugging, stroking, and torturing me while he worshipped me. The decadent pulsation excited me beyond reason.

"Open your eyes, Aria."

His voice was thick with command. I loved how erotic my name sounded as it fell from his lips. His eyes burned me with need as he seduced me into submission. His hands, just moments ago at my waist, effortlessly lifted me onto the counter. I felt like I was floating. I read his mind and shivered with anticipation of what was to come.

Lifting my arms, he removed the inconvenient clothing that had become a nuisance to us both. He played my breasts. They recognized his touch. His thumbs gently coasted over the nipples, the pressure increasing until they were painful, hardened tips. Still, his eyes never left mine. He loved to watch my reactions. I was equally sucked in by desire.

"Absolute perfection."

The words were a decree that unraveled and consumed me. I marinated in their implication. I arched my back while he loved each one and sucked the aching nubs. He reached for my hair, pulling the elastic from my curls until they fell free. As he tugged my hair back with a firm grip, his lips vibrated against my throat.

"Do you know what I want?"

"I do."

My voice trailed to a whisper and my eyelids grew heavy with lust. Though I could barely reason, I knew with all certainty that I wanted this. I wanted him. He eased my grief and brought me more joy than I imagined a person could bring.

"Say it."

"You want me ... to want you."

"And do you?"

His voice was powerful, the effect immediate. He confidently coaxed the ache inside of me. It fed his thirst to conquer and made him drunk to know that I wanted him. There was only one thing I could say that could satisfy us both.

"I want you to make love to me. I want you to make me forget my name while you make me scream yours."

He dined on the throaty urgency of my words and feasted on my request. He froze. His stare was steeled with intensity and it bore deep into my heart.

"Damn, I missed you woman!"

Impatiently he shucked his clothes. I drank in all of what the world appreciated, but for now, was only mine. His solid chest. His thick shoulders. The sharp vee that compelled me to look further down until I salivated for what was to come. I watched as the veins on both sides of his neck pulsated in concert with my need. I closed my eyes. The anticipation was delicious and I couldn't bear the wait. I wanted it. That cataclysmic first connection of skin on skin. All of my senses were on overdrive from scent to sound. The unmistakable sound of ripping foil sent an unexpected shiver through me as it predicted what was to come.

He leaned into me and my nipples electrified when we connected. His large hands slid beneath my bottom as he lifted and pulled my jeans off. They were thrown to the floor, sacrificed to his lust. His needy fingers bruised my bottom as he roughly pulled me against him. Chest to breast. Heat to hard.

He demanded my mouth, lifting me while I wrapped my legs around his waist. With accurate precision, he positioned himself and I sank into the sweet burn. He controlled his invasion and made a deep slide against my soaked entrance. I ached from the stretch. A graveled, guttural moan escaped him as he carried me into the bedroom. I was impaled on him. Every step teased my arousal and when I felt the soft material at my back, he masterfully met my every need with regulated measure. With each stroke, I soared with craving want and pleasured pain. He showered my body, mind, and soul with equal parts of love and lust. The obsessive taste he'd developed to be inside of me compelled him thrust after thrust until I shattered, my consciousness exploding like a brilliant sun. He followed quickly behind, never slowing the rhythm until we both plummeted over the edge of euphoria.

Suspended in time by invisible threads, both of us dangled in the breeze of satisfaction. He held me tight and stayed inside of me until we both began to breathe with some semblance of normalcy. I never wanted to move from this moment. I never wanted him to leave. I wanted to stay connected exactly like this forever. My mind couldn't focus on one feeling. There were too many of them from which I never wanted to stray and all of them were wonderful.

The sheet was clean and crisp, and wonderfully cool against my heated skin. I floated in contentment, my thoughts dangling in a mid-air state of gratification. Declan held on to me and gently rolled until we were side by side. His eyes were soft, the corners relaxed. I saw and felt his happiness. His voice gently caressed me as I looked into the warmth of his eyes.

"I love you, Aria."

The words cascaded over me in a cool stream. I should have felt relief, but fear penetrated my satiated mind. Re-entering reality quickly, I looked into his eyes, searching for any disingenuous hints. I found none. I saw only sincerity in his handsome features, but I struggled with belief. *He loved me?*

It would be foolish for a woman like me to *not* be cautiously optimistic. *How many women had he dated? How many had been in his bed? Was I the only woman who'd heard those words? The first woman? He was a man of the world and I was a woman of the ... STOP!*

I couldn't allow my overcharged anxiety to ruin this moment. His expression was soft and tender. I reeked with doubt and he looked as if he could read my thoughts.

"Stop thinking so hard, because it's true. I know what's probably going through that beautiful mind ... but it's true." His tone was soft and tender, blanketing my trepidation with heartfelt honesty. "I've never said it before. Never."

Doubt tugged at my lingering thread of disbelief, trying its best to unravel my optimism. I couldn't look at him. I needed a moment and broke our connection by casting my eyes down. He refused to allow me to twist his words and intent by lifting my chin and forcing me to look at him.

"I want you to listen to me. Just for a minute, okay?"

My slight nod was all the permission he needed to continue.

"I've never said those words before because I've never felt this way before. About *anyone.*"

I scoffed, causing him to frown. "Madison Avenue might own my looks, but only you have my heart."

All I could manage was a weak smile because words escaped me. He was telling the truth. Every emotion I had left rushed straight to my heart. I refused to speak because I knew that my voice would betray the enormity of his impact. His confession breached my carefully constructed wall of rationale. But then, love isn't rational. It's a battering ram smashing cynicism and logic. If I tried to figure it out, a litany of *what ifs* would come crashing into my head. All I wanted to do was savor this moment. Commit it to memory. Etch it in my heart.

I pressed into him, snuggling my ear against his chest. It was comfortably quiet and in the silence, I listened to the sound of his heartbeat. The solid rhythm coaxed me into a new sense of security. The feeling was unfamiliar, scary, and ... *wonderful*.

He held me tightly against him, making me feel treasured and cherished. I savored it. Everything else—*the future, the unknowns, the what-ifs*—was irrelevant and as the moon's silver light marked the passing of our hours together, nothing else mattered. No one else existed.

Just Declan and me.

CHAPTER
Fifteen

Aria

"This is serious, huh?"

The baritone-laced question interrupted my thoughts. I chewed nervously on my bottom lip and looked over at the man whose physical appearance commanded the attention of women all over the world. As much as I should have been enjoying the realization that he was mine, only one thought whirled in my head on a non-stop loop: *what would my mother think of him?*

"I promise. I'll be on my best behavior."

Amusement laced his tone while lifting the corners of his mouth into a patronizing grin. Once again, it seemed he could read my thoughts. He threaded his fingers through mine and gave my hand a reassuring squeeze. The knots in my empty stomach twisted mercilessly. I couldn't believe I had agreed to this.

Declan was about to meet my mother.

I still don't know how it had happened. It had started out so innocently. Just a normal phone call. She asked how work was. I said *good.* I asked how she was. She said *good.* Normal stuff. The next few minutes were filled with our typical generalizations and the normal catching up that a mother and daughter do all the time.

And then Declan walked into the room.

I didn't think anything of it, really. He kissed the top of my head and said he was going for a run. And then I was hit with rapid-fire questions.

"Who was that?"

"Um. My boyfriend?" I answered in more of a question than a comment. My response was the "matter of fact" way you use when you're trying to avoid a subject.

"Boyfriend? Really? You mentioned going out a few times, and might even have said you were seeing someone, but you left out the "boyfriend" part. Soooooo ...?

Her tone made me roll my eyes. "So?"

"Is he nice?"

"I think so. You'd probably like him."

"Great! I'll meet you two for lunch next Saturday. Normal time. Same spot. Gotta go!"

And there it was. That fast. She was slick, my mother. I swear. I never saw it coming. It wasn't that I didn't want her to meet him, or vice versa, I just ... *Oh God!* I don't know. I guess I couldn't keep him to myself forever. It had been a long time since I had a boyfriend. And she was overprotective. And inquisitive. And now she was meeting him. And I was as nervous as a teenager. All I could do was hope for the best. *Sheesh!*

I was in a daze the entire drive. Oblivious to everything. I didn't even notice when the car stopped. I looked up and we were in the parking lot of The Fisherman's Inn. It felt like we got there in under a minute.

I stared out the windshield at the sign above the door and my stomach did another tiny flip. He squeezed my hand to get my attention.

"Time to face the music."

I looked over at the playful expression on his face. He rolled his eyes at me.

"I wonder what she'll think?"

I frowned. "Shut up! Now you're just playing with me."

"Of course I am! I'm trying to get you to lighten up!"

"It's not working."

He leaned across the console, taking my chin in his hand. His kiss took me by surprise. It wasn't the reassuring peck I expected. It was hot and deep, lasting far too long to be meeting my mother in a minute. But it was enough to take my breath and momentarily erase my thoughts.

"Now, stop it. I promise to be on my best behavior. I won't even try anything funny under the table—with you or your mom."

I smacked his arm and smiled. The mental image of Declan mistaking my leg for my mother's leg for mine lightened my mood. "You wouldn't dare."

He roguishly wiggled his eyebrows. "I wouldn't. Promise. Maybe." The one corner of his mouth snagged devilishly. "But your mom might like it."

"Oh my God, Declan!" I choked on the laugh that sprung from my chest. It eased the band of tension that had been wrapping itself around me. Just the thought of him grabbing my mom … *Ewww!*

He exited the car and walked around to open my door. Hand in hand, we walked up to the restaurant while anticipation bubbled in my stomach. He ushered me in and again took my hand as we headed toward the hostess station. He'd confided to me just before we left the house that this was also one of his favorite places.

The Fisherman's Inn had spectacular gardens inside and out. Plush and green, they blended in with the natural landscape. I always requested seating at the windows, especially one table in particular that had the best vantage point of the pond and waterfall. When I was little, we always stopped here on our way home from vacation. I could have looked out the window for hours watching the water caress the rocks as it cascaded around the enormous assortment of flowers. To the little girl in me, it seemed magical and I mentally transported myself there many times. I had so many good memories of coming here with my parents. It was also a favorite of my mother's, so she and I met here once a month to catch up.

My mother. The dictionary was filled with too many adjectives to describe her. *Thoughtful. Over-protective. Spirited.* One thing was for sure: she was resilient. She bounced back from adversity quicker than anyone I knew, but the one thing that she still struggled with was losing my dad. She mourned his loss in a quiet way and I wasn't sure if I could picture her moving on. They had been together since they were teenagers; she was trying to make her way without him, but it was hard. Someone said that time heals all wounds, but I don't agree. I think time only makes the wound easier to bear. I could only hope that Mom would find herself again. Keeping busy helped. She had thrown herself into what she loved—flowers, especially roses. She could turn a bunch of flowers into a stunning arrangement. It had been a natural fit when she went to work at a local florist. She relished the hustle and bustle and her shop was always busy. It was so good to see her doing something that made her happy. When my father was alive, she had met his every need. As his illness progressed, he relied more heavily on her and I watched her vibrant personality gradually disappear. There was very little of it left as he became bitter from the loss of his independence. Dad's incapacity rendered him powerless over even his most personal needs. Bickering and contention disfigured the loving relationship my parents had shared. He grew angry, misdirecting all of that negative energy at my mother. Although she understood the root of his contemptuous moods, the knowledge didn't make it easier to bear. He resented her help, and toward the end, he became harsh, indignant, and depressed. It was a blessing when he gained his angel wings, but it still left a hole in our hearts. It had been months since he had passed and I was proud of her for putting the puzzle pieces of her identity back together. And now I was about to let her see how my own pieces were coming together. She was sitting exactly where I thought she'd be and as she locked eyes with me, I swallowed the lump in my throat.

CHAPTER
Sixteen

Declan

I spotted her instantly. The family resemblance was unmistakable. Though her hair was shorter and her face slightly fuller, the similarities between Aria and her mother were evident. She stood as we approached the table, embraced Aria, and reached out to me with a slender hand. She and Aria wore the same smile.

"Hello, you must be Declan. I'm Jeannie Cole. It's a pleasure to meet you."

"Thank you." I returned the smile. Aria slid across the booth seat and I took my place beside her. Jeannie positioned herself across from us.

"Aria speaks highly of you, Declan. It's nice to see a smile on her face."

I momentarily glanced sideways and caught the blush creeping into Aria's cheeks before responding to Jeannie's comment. "Good to hear. I think Aria's pretty special, too."

"I was glad they had our favorite spot available." A twinkle danced in Jeannie's eyes as she volleyed her gaze between Aria and me. "Whenever we've come here, from the time she was little, this has always been Aria's favorite spot."

"What she doesn't know is that it's my favorite seat as well." Aria's brows shot up inquisitively. "My mother used to bring my brother and me to this restaurant when we were boys. It was the last stop on our vacations. The toy train that rides the ceiling fascinated us. I think my mom liked looking at the gardens."

"Oh, so you vacationed on the Eastern Shore?"

"Yes, ma'am. Every year for as long as I can remember. It was the only place our family ever went."

"Does your family still vacation here?"

"No, ma'am. My mom passed away several years ago. Cancer. My dad wasn't in the picture. My brother, Carter, he and his wife live in the mountains. Deep Creek Lake. He's a State Trooper and she's a teacher."

Aria squeezed my hand as a frown played at her mother's lips. "I'm sorry about your mother."

"Me, too. She was a pretty special lady. She would have loved my house at the beach."

"Aria told me about your house. She said it's beautiful."

I stole a brief look at Aria. She wore an easy smile and I felt my shoulders relax. "I love it and I spend as much time here as I can ... especially because I get to see your daughter when I'm here."

Jeannie smiled. "I'm sure it's beautiful." Her expression softened as she looked at us both before continuing. "Does your brother like it?"

"I haven't been able to coax him away from Deep Creek yet, but summer's coming. Lacey will be off for a few months and I think she's convinced Carter to come down."

"Are you two very close?"

"Yes, ma'am. I travel a lot so we don't see each other as much as we'd like, but we talk about once a week." It was the truth. Carter kept me grounded. My life had changed dramatically with notoriety. My brother kept the fame from giving me a distorted view. I could always rely on his honesty. He was my best friend.

Aria sat quietly while her mother continued with another question.

"You mention that you travel a lot. I was surprised when she said she was dating a model. I have to admit, I'm just a little uneasy about that."

"Mom!" Aria protested. I moved my hand between them in a settle down motion and looked at her.

"It's okay. Your mom has a point." I locked eyes with Jeannie. "You're right to be concerned. I can't imagine what you thought when she told you she was dating me. I don't have the most polished reputation, especially if you read what's in the tabloids. But I will tell you this: Aria's the kind of woman that doesn't buy into all that crap."

Pride filled her mother's expression. "I agree with you and I'm proud of her for that."

"I had been making tentative plans when I met her. Since then I've been trying to solidify them. I'd like a more stable life. I'm tired of all the traveling and I've grown tired of the fake people that go along with the lifestyle. Aria's the best thing that's happened to me in a long time."

The look on Aria's face was confirmation that she felt the same.

"He has an impressive plan and has been putting together a proposal for the executives at his agency."

"True. And you've been a big help letting me bounce ideas off you." I kissed the side of her head before continuing. "I've made a considerable amount of money and I'd like to do something positive with it. The agencies are always looking for new talent. Ocean City, Bethany, Fenwick, and Rehoboth are inundated with young people working summer jobs. They're the perfect selection pool for models. I'd like to open a private studio. Somewhere to vet new talent before sending them off to New York. It would give me a place to scout them and it would give them a place to prepare for what happens in the industry. I know what the agencies are looking for. The East Coast needs an office. Somewhere between Florida and New York. I think Ocean City is a perfect place to connect new talent with a reputable agency. I'd like to fill that need."

Jeannie smiled at me. There was no doubt that she was pleased by what she heard, but the dissertation I provided for her mother seemed to have weathered Aria. She looked worn from the scrutiny, but Jeannie seemed delighted.

"It sounds like you have a solid plan, Declan. I'm impressed." She turned her attention to Aria. "Sweetie, you're being awfully quiet. Did I embarrass you?" Amusement laced her tone.

"Mom …" She rolled her eyes. "You have too many questions. It was a little third degree-ish. So … does he pass?" The question was filled with a lighthearted tone.

"Yes. With flying colors. Now stop worrying and let's eat!"

CHAPTER
Seventeen

Marisol

*D*amn it!

Marisol placed her finger on the screen. It did little to erase the cause of her anger. The display flaunted her latest fixation. *Declan.* He was, once again, in the company of the woman who was fast becoming her nemesis.

In their last conversation, the worthless investigator related the details of the woman with whom Declan chose to keep company. Her name was revealed as one Aria Cole. She was a washed-up hair-stylist who had found her inner masculinity. A butchy girl whose most recent companions before Declan were a hammer and screw-driver. A woman who would be better suited for some buck-toothed, beer-guzzling redneck from the backwoods town of *Disenchantia.* Instead, she was trying to sink her screws into one of the world's most eligible bachelors. *What the hell does he see in her?*

Marisol's phone vibrated with a text indicating that this particu-lar photo, and several others, had been taken at a restaurant some-where near the Chesapeake Bay. Following the text was another photo of a third party. An older woman. One more photo featuring Declan and the two women laughing completed the report. The fire inside of her burned hotter the more she thought about how close his new little group was becoming. Originating from tinder of possessive hostility, the burn continued and had been building ever since she had learned of Aria.

A-ree-a.

Ugh!

She had to think of something. Apparently the man was having a premature midlife crisis. He hadn't even been answering her attempts to contact him. And she had been trying. Text, phone, and email. More than one. Several, in fact. No matter how hard she tried. The razor-sharp sting of truth slapped her across her expertly cosmeticized face. He was avoiding her.

Unacceptable!

She slowly paced, mentally searching through a sea of ideas to separate Declan and his newest plaything. Although work had brought him to New York since she'd learned of Aria, none of their projects cooperated with her desire to get him alone *and* to get them together. She had gone out of her way in attempts to intercept him. She frequented his hangouts, injected herself into his social circles, and even hunted down—just dropping by—business meetings where his presence might be required. Nothing. Inquiries proved fruitless when, time and again, she learned that he either hadn't made an appearance or she had just missed him. She decided that, as usual, in order for something to happen, *she* had to be the one to make it happen.

A well-placed phone call to a favorite client and an adventurous night spent in the man's bed proved to be the perfect recipe to get Declan exactly where she wanted him. Her well-played sexual talents resulted in having him back in New York within a few days. Riding the putrid old man got her an underwear contract where she and Declan would be working closely together.

Closely.

Together.

She wore her manipulation with pride. There was no way she

would let this inadequate little sand flea usurp her place in Declan's life. The audacity that this woman had in even trespassing on ground that she'd claimed astounded her. There was no way that even a bikini-clad beach whore whose head was either in the sand or up her own ass wouldn't have known about the relationship she had with Declan. *Unless they didn't have magazines in her podunk little town. Or she couldn't read.*

Marisol gave the photo of Declan and Aria a second look. She would simply take back what was rightfully hers and kick the *hija de puta arrogante* back to the dunes she crawled out of. Just looking at her made her want to wretch. Obviously, it wasn't because she felt threatened by her. Her ire was because Declan seemed pleased by the woman and he was only allowed pleasure when in *her* company. Not with that *estupida elephante!*

Enough was enough! As she glanced at herself in the mirror, she tossed her head back. Gleaming brilliantly in the filtered afternoon sun, her hair cascaded gracefully and magnificently over her shoulders then trailed down the curve of her back. Tilting her head up, she ran a fingernail down over her slender throat and continued until the pointed tip stabbed her nipple. *This* was what he really needed. *She* was what he truly wanted.

A sardonic smile, one that couldn't reach the Botoxed corners of her eyes, revealed an introspection that was more than pleasant. *She* was the most beautiful woman in the world and not just in her own eyes. According to the market and the media, there was no one to whom she could compare. One such source was quoted as saying "… if Cleopatra was the face that launched a thousand ships, Marisol Franzi was the face that launched billions of dollars." Perhaps it was time that she impressed upon Declan exactly how lucky he was. She could have anyone she wanted, but she wanted him. It was imperative to her agenda that she be linked with a man who had looks and power. His looks were nearly comparable to hers and once she cleaned up a few minor details, she had the background and experience in manipulative tactics to make them both powerful. He merely needed to recognize his good fortune. Once his head cleared of the dirty sand—where he had been spending far too much time—he could come play with her. With the finer things. In the finer things. And she would play with him as well. She had only one rule: No one else was allowed to play with her things.

CHAPTER
Eighteen

Aria

I have a tendency to worry. I don't know why. Drama's not my style and I'm always accused of thinking too deeply. I've been known to slightly obsess. I care too much. Again, I don't know why. It's just who I am and I most definitely thought too deeply, as well as became slightly obsessed, about this whole *mom meets boyfriend* thing. But today? It couldn't have gone more perfectly. Mom was impressed. Her attitude and body language proved it. She's usually much more cynical about people than I am, but with the charming Declan Sinclair? She fell in love with him. *But then, what woman wouldn't?*

Declan and I barely spoke on the drive home. A relaxed storm started to build along the way, both inside and outside of the car. As I stared out of the window, he reached over and placed his hand on my knee. It was meant to be a sweet, comforting gesture to assure me that he was as happy as I was about the outcome of the event. But his touch did more than comfort me, it turned me on. I'd been a keg of dynamite waiting for a match all day. His touch ignited the fuse. I placed my wrist over his hand and pinched my sundress with two fingers. As I pushed his hand up my thigh, I raised the hemline.

His head snapped in my direction and he gave me a puzzled look. His gaze then slipped down to my bare leg and I immediately saw the corner of his mouth hook with pleasure. He wasn't expecting this, but he didn't realize that the impact of stress, good or bad, could transfer at any moment. I was sure that he'd seen it before. It was like a surprise party or when a person laughs and cries at the same time. My anxiety-filled mental strain had now transferred to sexual tension.

He moved his hand, resting it beneath the connection where my leg met my hip. The rhythm of his breathing changed, increasing as desire began to sink in. As his eyes volleyed between my thigh and the road, I shifted my weight to my hip and leaned in his direction. My legs spread slightly with the action. We were the only car approaching the traffic light and when the car came to a stop, I seductively slinked the remaining length of my dress over my skin. I let the material drape across my lap, hinting at what was beneath and hiding my rising need. His gaze hardened to an intensified stare. He was used to doing what he wanted, when he wanted, but he had to wait. *Poor baby!*

I enjoyed the game and his distress. His look turned into a glare when the light changed to green and he had to tear his eyes away to watch the road. It was the perfect opportunity for me to see the effect of my playfulness and I wasn't disappointed. His slacks were strained across his lap and the tenting appeared to be painful.

For the entire drive home, he let me control my vehicle-restricted burlesque show as he struggled to keep his eyes on the highway. I massaged the area across his lap and reveled in seeing the effect. At one point, I thought his jaw would crack from the strain. He refused to look at me or say a word, but his behavior revealed his lusty thoughts. I took it one step further once I knew we were only minutes from the house and lifted his hand, placing it under the slippery material of my dress. I pressed his hand until his fingers cupped my sex. Initially resistant, his hand relaxed and he explored beneath my panties. Now it was my turn to catch my breath as his cool hand met my wet heat. He slowly slid his fingers through the soft groove, teasing me when he stilled them in a position that intensified the aching pulsation. His actions demanded my focus, insistent for my attention in a way that made me neglect any other thoughts. My head fell back against the headrest as he branded my most tender part with his fingertips.

Lost in sensation, my eyes flew open when the car came to a stop. The looks we exchanged were powerful. Mine: needy. His: predatory. The intensity in his eyes connected with his actions and he increased the pressure of his hand. I was a victim to the rip current of lust that rippled through me. His lips were a tight line. A flash of ferocity electrified his stare.

"You'll pay for this."

The threat of retribution cracked through the hoarse baritone that crept under his breath. It exposed his hunger from deep in his chest, but instead of making me fearful it excited me. I sat still and silent as he pulled his hand back angrily and flipped the hem of my dress so that the garment fell back to its original position near my ankles. He got out of the car. He firmly shoved his door to a near slam before walking around to my side. One small click and my door flew open. The change in temperature from the inside heat to an ocean breeze skated along the surface of my skin, leaving goose bumps in its wake. His outstretched hand demanded mine as he pulled me into captivity. His position forced me so close to him that there was barely room for a breath to pass between us. With his other hand, he put the key in the door. His eyes never left mine and I was caught in an undertow of passion. The feeling commanded me to look at him and as he pushed the door open an aura of power pulsated behind the gold flecks hidden in his deep brown eyes.

"Inside, Aria. Now."

My mind detonated at the eerie calm in his command. It sucked away any oxygen connecting my thoughts. I was drowning in desire, tethered to his hand, my mind anchoring to his intimate edict. The door had barely closed behind us when I found myself nearly catapulted against the wall. The action took my breath and I was crushed between his heat and the cool surface at my back. His lips came crashing down on mine as he yanked the strapless top from my breasts. His starched white shirt now exposed from under the lapel of his jacket morphed from a gentlemanly garment used to impress my mother to a chafing sex toy. The material rubbed my bare skin until my nipples grew sensitive and hardened. He pressed into me, making me fully aware of his fully afflicted need.

He wasted no time, neglecting to undress himself or me. He merely yanked up the bottom of my dress and took what he wanted. With an impatient hand, he slipped his fingers through my panties and ripped the silky material free. The motion against my crotch was startling and I became oblivious to sight and sound, choosing instead to simply feel. The last sound I heard was the rip of metal as he pulled down his zipper. Without warning, he savagely entered me, simultaneously wrapping his powerful hands around my thighs to open me fully. I had barely caught my breath when he issued the next thrust and the fiery friction took me to a new level of sexual hunger. Fully inside of me, my body perversely welcomed the burning assault as he rode me mercilessly.

I savored every moment of this unfamiliar excitement as Declan took full possession. His demanding mouth never left mine as he claimed what he owned. His lovemaking was uncharitable as he sent my entire being a message—*I was his*. There would be no going back to sweet impressions. Somehow while traveling from Kent Island to Ocean City we'd graduated from that phase of our relationship. I was no longer an awkward girl but a wicked woman and he was proud of his part in the transformation. He had walked me through the stages of lovemaking and in this new twist, I happily surrendered to his dominance. Before he'd been patient and sweet. There was nothing sweet about this. I had opened Pandora's Box by teasing him and what I received in return was Declan's insatiable appetite. He wanted to be in every part of my life. He was kind, but this love was different. It was demanding.

I craved the new high as it hurled me toward unfamiliar heights. My fingers sunk into his shoulders as I struggled for air. I struggled for consciousness as I approached unexperienced elevations. I took one last wisp of air, then exploded with pleasure. Silent screams went unvoiced as my body detonated. Sparkling erotic fireworks, more brilliant than any I'd previously experienced, flashed before my eyes. His hungry mouth swallowed my non-vocal cries as he refused to let the fire fizzle out. He selfishly took everything until there was nothing left, pushing me again to the edge until he'd had his fill. A roar escaped as he quickened his pace, his release blazing inside of me. When it was over, I fell limp against his chest as both of our bodies begged for air.

The high slowly faded and we descended with overworked muscles. My legs were limp as he carried me to his bed with them still wrapped around his waist. Our physical connection was still intact while our souls welded in ways we didn't expect. The forging was potent. Our love was invincible. Only something more powerful could break the bond. Confident that nothing stronger existed, I realized that this day would change everything about us, because it changed the dynamic *of* us.

Yellow is a happy color. It silently crept through the cracks in my sleepy eyelids and greeted me with its welcoming cheer. As the morning sunlight grew from a peek to a ray, the rhythmic song of the ocean rocked my sated soul. I slowly drifted toward consciousness to the call of the rhythm of the waves. Repetitive lyrics of seagulls roused me further still, while the whistle of faint ocean breezes meshed with the beating of my heart. A symphony of happiness crescendoed through me as the struggle to open my eyes lessened.

I fought the residual soreness from the events of the previous night, as my mind grew more focused. My limbs were heavy and I debated slipping back into my slumbered state. The ache between my legs was deliciously sore and I tingled all over at the memory. I looked down at Declan's arm draped possessively over my midsection and when I tried to move it, he tightened his hold. Instead of it making me feel claustrophobic, I felt loved and protected. My unobstructed view of him allowed for a perfect vision of his sculpted back and arms. Every muscle, from his neck to his calves, was tight and I enjoyed myself as I lingered appreciatively on each one. My gaze traveled upward to his profile. One cheek was on the pillow, the other was facing me. It was chiseled and fierce. His jaw was firmly set, even in sleep. The image was powerful and definitely reflected his reputation as "the man with the iron stare."

And he belongs to me.

As I watched him peacefully sleep, I was sucked into the mesmerizing vortex of the large tattoo covering his back. It was as unique as Declan. Inquisitiveness invited me to explore by lightly tracing the inked circles and swirls with the tip of my finger.

"Good morning."

"Mmm hmm."

The corduroy sound of his morning voice defined him: rough, yet velvety.

"It's time to wake up."

"No it isn't."

His eyes stayed closed as I intimately wrapped my fingers around his semi-soft skin. It responded to my touch and grew increasingly stiff as I slowly began to stroke.

"Aren't you hungry? The last time you ate something was with my mother." My hoarse whisper suggested something more than food. He caught my wrist and pulled me against him.

"Right now your mother is the furthest thing from my mind."

It only took him a second to adjust our positions and the sudden movement surprised me. I was beneath him and with an amused grin, he looked into my eyes.

"You shouldn't wake a sleeping bear, sweetheart."

Pinned beneath him, I was at his mercy. My body responded on its own as his hand slid to the inside of my thighs. He settled himself between my legs and glided into me. The handsome, amused grin I'd noticed just moments before switched to playfully evil. It was obvious that he was enjoying having me at his mercy. He nudged my cheek. His low growl against my ear caused ripples of pleasure to travel to my core.

"You know what happens, don't you, sweetheart? Once bears are awake they have insatiable appetites."

CHAPTER
Nineteen

Declan

New York City. Icy, bitter cold winters and concrete-stench heat in the summer. It's been my home away from home for many years. It is also home to Bella Matrix, Inc., the epicenter of America's fashion industry and my prime connection to the city and my agent, Blake Matthews. Most of my work takes me to different locations, but this particular shoot is in the heart of the theatre district. After much prompting, Aria agreed to come with me. I had seen her at work and she decided to reciprocate. Having her with me made this trip an easy one.

I'd never before invited a woman to come with me on a photo shoot. Frankly, I didn't know what reaction she would have when she saw the details involved. It would look like a totally narcissistic environment because once I arrived, all of the attention would be on me and the other models. Hair, make-up, and clothing—it could give the impression of complete self-indulgence.

Unlike some models, my look was my brand. I made a conscious effort to be closely involved in the process and marketing of the *Declan Sinclair* business. I was very opinionated about how my look was projected and perceived and I had worked long and hard to earn the right to do so. When I came into modeling, men weren't featured. I was blazing the trail for the guys that came after me.

Although the client dictated the final work product, I had it written into my contracts that I had first option of what they were shown. If I was displeased in any way, whether it was lighting, pose, or projection, I would express that to the photographer and we'd work together to correct it. It had taken a lot of years to pull off my reputation for excellence and I had earned the respect of the professionals I worked with. There were a select few that reflected similar work ethics and were gifted and talented in their own right that kept me in my number one spot. This ensured future success and translated into sales. A numbers game. It was that simple. I wanted my world with Aria. She knew the real me, but wasn't familiar with the man in the ads. I wanted her to be able to discern between the two.

I woke early to go to the hotel gym. When I returned, she was still sleeping. Her dark hair was fanned on the pillow beneath her cheek as I bent to kiss her. The sight of Aria caused my heart to respond in a way that was foreign to me. Just looking at her took away the command and control that I'd always been able to maintain. Her sweet and easy nature made it so easy to be with her, but as I stripped off my sweaty clothes, sweet thoughts were not what crossed my mind. I needed a cold shower.

***

I felt her before I heard her. The shower had more than enough room for two. I was leaning into the spray of water when Aria approached me from behind and kissed my shoulder.

"Good morning."

I turned to face her. "Good morning. To what do I owe this pleasure?"

"I missed you and I wanted to start off the day in a good way." She looked up at me as the water began to soak through her hair. I put my hands in it, tilting her face up for a morning kiss.

"My day always starts off in a good way when you're with me."
I kissed her wet lips. "I don't have much time. A car will be coming
for me in about an hour or so."

She returned my kiss. A coy smile appeared as though she
didn't hear me. She ran her hands slowly from my shoulders and
down toward my hips. My body responded to her kisses, licks, and
teasing bites. They tested my control and I disregarded the internal
warning that I was definitely going to be late for work. I loved this
side of Aria. She had grown much bolder as she became more confident in her sexuality. I loved the little tigress that believed she was in
authority. Her hands were silky with body wash; she glided them
from my glutes to my thighs, increasing and decreasing the pressure.
I silently warred between taking her against the wall or letting her
have her way. She pressed her body against mine.

"I see someone got their workout in this morning. Your muscles
look so big. They feel ... so hard. Every ... one ... of ... them."

Her voice was seductively smoky and a deep groan escaped me.
My Aria. This little jungle cat apparently wanted to play. I leaned
back, allowing her full access.

"You know, Bear, being a hairstylist all those years made me
particular about grooming. Are you familiar with the term
manscaping?"

Her blue-gray eyes shined with adventure. I nodded. A lump
formed in my throat and my tongue thickened. Words wouldn't
come as I looked at the razor in her hand. She lathered me, slowly
stroking to get the full effect, and looked up into my eyes.

"Trust me?"

One eyebrow cocked as she cupped me in her palm. I cleared
my throat.

"Implicitly." I took the hand with the razor and gripped her
wrist, lifted it to my lips, and kissed the back of it. She smiled a
wicked smile, lifting the corner of her mouth.

"Spread ..."

I did as ordered. I couldn't move—hell, I couldn't breathe—as the cold metal slid across my skin. It was the most sensual experience, but also invoked excitement and fear.

When she had completed her task, she gave me a smoldering look while the water washed away the remnants of soap.

"I think I like it." She pointed to the shower seat. "Sit."

I obeyed the command. The hard evidence of my excitement was apparent the moment I sat down. The water had dampened her hair to ebony and it contrasted dramatically against her fair skin; she looked like a goddess. My hands nearly twitched with the urge to explore, but instead I sat back to enjoy my view. She looked up and down as if she'd created a masterpiece, then reached down and teased me with her fingers, playing with the smoothness left behind from her labor. *Oh hell!*

One leg, then the other, came around my waist as she positioned herself. As she straddled me, her full breasts rubbed against my chest. Her hands wove through my hair. She pulled, forcing me to look into her eyes. A wicked spark flashed through them. I itched to slip inside of her, but she reached beside me to the shampoo. She massaged my neck and head and worked a lather into my scalp. Her motions were sensuous. The touch of her fingertips was erotic. My self-control was being tested.

I could no longer resist pulling her close. Water trickled down my face as it rested against her wet, glistening breasts. I took one moist nub into my mouth, then the other. Her lids fluttered as a moan escaped. I lingered, enjoying the taste and feel of her. She pulled my head back. Her voice was ragged, but her gaze blazed with excitement.

"I know how important *appearance* is to you. I wanted to help."

I laughed. "I'm not advertising that part of me." She responded with a mischievous grin. "So, are you pleased with your work?"

She pushed herself away and struck a provocative pose. She was a beautifully naked artist perusing a canvas. Tilting her head back and forth, she played the part.

As the imaginary clock ticked in my head, I realized the game had to end. Hell bent on taking her hard and fast, I narrowed my eyes and reached for her. With a hand on each round cheek, I stood and yanked her against me. She pushed against my chest and gave me a devilish grin. Slowly, she slid to her knees. When she reached the floor, she looked up at me through thick, damp lashes and licked her lips. I caught my breath as she gripped me. The sight of her on her knees and the unfamiliar feeling of her fingers against my bare flesh nearly made me explode.

"You asked if I'm pleased?" Her tongue traced the length of me as her seductive tone mixed with a vibrating groan. She looked up and gave me one last, devouring look.

"You're mouthwatering."

CHAPTER
Twenty

Aria

Declan's photo shoot was taking place in The New Amsterdam Theatre in the heart of New York's theatre district. This was my first time in the city and I was filled with child-like excitement. I was nearly giddy as we approached Broadway and 42nd Street. I was equally excited when we walked into a piece of history.

I took a seat about ten rows back from the stage. Declan told me that the entire shoot would be done on the stage. I set my briefcase down. I had planned on making myself inconspicuous while doing some paperwork, but I was on sensory overload. The architecture was overwhelming and every time I tried to put pen to paper, something in my peripheral vision tore me away from the task at hand.

I soaked in my surroundings like a sponge. I was completely enchanted by the attention to detail that had been exercised in the restoration. The beautiful paintings and ornate carvings were absolutely breathtaking. I wanted to feel the lush, deep purple curtains beneath my fingers. They were so beautiful that they begged to be touched. A memory flashed through my mind. When I was a little girl, I used to watch old movies on television with my mom. I would wait in the kitchen with her as she popped popcorn just before one of her favorite movies was scheduled to air. We would cozy up in a chair together and share the bowl as we watched. Color became a guessing game as we speculated on the tones of the actors' hair and clothes, as well as the furniture. When we watched the old movie about Ziegfeld's life, we had imagined what color and material the theatre's curtains were made of; and now, here I was, in the place from the movie. There was no way that I could just sit in my seat and do paperwork.

I walked down to the orchestra area and looked up at the ceiling. The artistry was fascinating. I could have walked with my head in the air for hours. Because of the type of work that I did, I was in awe of the skill and imagination of the craftsmen who had restored the theatre. Ziegfeld would most definitely have approved. Because of their attention to detail, The New Amsterdam Theatre remained one of the oldest surviving venues of the original Broadway district. Remembering my mom's love for all things from the 1930's and 1940's, I discreetly took pictures with my phone.

I was interrupted by voices and slowly made my way back to my seat. People were on stage arranging furniture and lighting. Declan walked out from the side. The curtain had been pushed back just a bit while they were prepping him for the photos, but not enough that I could see the details. A bevy of people surrounded him; hair stylists and make-up artists moved in a carefully choreographed dance to enhance his looks. I had just taken my seat when he scanned the audience to find me and gave me an indecent look. All I could do was stare.

CHAPTER
Twenty-One

Declan

I shifted in my chair while they did my hair and make-up so that I could watch Aria. She walked up and down the aisles taking pictures with her phone. There was a look of wonder on her face. Her excitement about being in New York was infectious. I was seeing the city with a new perspective through my sweet girl's eyes. *Her eyes!* I could only imagine the spectrum of color changes in her beautiful blues.

I called out to her and gave a very brief introduction of the staff. She looked like a kid in a candy store as her eyes took in everyone and everything. She didn't know that I'd been watching her from backstage. I was feeling overprotective for many reasons, but this morning there was one reason in particular.

It hadn't been confirmed to me, but I was told that Marisol was scheduled for this shoot. If that was true, she would be vicious. I'd seen her that way with other women. It never mattered to me before, but I knew that if she treated Aria with the same disdain I'd seen exhibited in the past, it wouldn't be pleasant. Combined with the fact that I'd been ignoring her, it could be ugly.

Aria was unaware that Marisol had called me. Numerous times.

Each time I had seen her name on the display, I hit the *decline* button
and ignored her. She'd always been a pain in my ass, but now that I
was in a relationship that I didn't want jeopardized, she was even
more so. She was a diva in the most extreme definition of the word.
She rode people to get what she wanted, literally and figuratively.
The press had labeled her *supermodel*, but she was more like *super-
bitch*. I didn't want Aria to know Marisol as anything other than a
name and a face. Marisol could be cunning, ruthless, and cruel while
flashing her million-dollar smile. She never made excuses or apologies. If something got in the way of what she wanted, she removed
the obstacle. The methods used were neither ethical nor moral, especially if another woman was involved. She'd do anything or screw
anyone to satisfy her desires. I didn't want Aria tainted by that evil.

Marisol and I had a love-hate relationship. It escalated the more
the press linked our names together. It had started at a party that
we'd both attended long ago. We were in a fragrance ad that had
taken on a life of its own. The marketing was amazing. It had been
filmed in the deep blue waters of the Mediterranean, off the coast of
Italy. The white swimsuits and blue contact lenses showcased our
bronzed skin. We played into the sexual roles that were coaxed on
by the film crew. Once the commercial aired, the press had a field
day. It was more successful than anyone could have dreamed. The
client wanted to show his appreciation by throwing a huge celebration party. During the party, Marisol decided that she would feed the
frenzy by making me one of her sexual conquests. Although I had
ignored her advances, she grew more persistent as the evening progressed. I overheard her making explicit comments that she was going to "ride me hard" and "be the best I'd ever had." It was laugha-
ble. And blatant. She had rubbed her ass and other body parts against
me every time she found me engaged in conversation. Her behavior
turned me off. It was whorish, crude, and vulgar. I found it unattrac-
tive, but after a few too many drinks I began to see her as just a piece
of ass. I was so drunk that I would have screwed her just because she
was that easy. I didn't care. I'd become that calloused. It was all

about me. I figured I'd find a closet or bathroom where I could take her, then go home and sleep it off. The plan changed when I received a phone call from the architect doing the renovation on my beach house.

I loved that house. It was the only thing that I did care about and I wanted to live there as soon as possible. He explained that all work had stopped. Something critical that involved a few thousand dollars needed both my personal attention and my signature. I didn't want anything to jeopardize the project so I knew what I had to do—and it didn't involve Marisol.

I went to the client, politely thanked him for a great party, and made my apologies to leave. When I left, I didn't say anything to Marisol. I didn't owe her an explanation. The plans she had for us were completely different than mine. She wanted to play up to the press, whereas I just wanted a quick way to relieve some stress. She could pick up some other random guy to nail that night.

I walked outside, gave the valet my keys, and took a deep breath to get some oxygen in my alcohol-soaked brain cells. I couldn't wait to trade this air for the salt-filled air of Ocean City. As I drove away, I noticed Marisol in my rearview mirror. Apparently, my change in plans didn't sit well with her. The look on her face told the tale.

My agent called me the next morning. Marisol had vented to him when I left. He told me that she didn't take my leaving well. She was so pissed that she cursed me in both English and Spanish. I laughed it off because I really didn't give a shit. I still didn't. But now, as I watched her walk in my direction, I knew that she was going be a problem.

CHAPTER
Twenty-Two

Aria

As I made myself comfortable, I saw another model heading toward Declan. She was easily recognizable. I think she was on at least one page of every magazine I owned. She was everything I wasn't: tall, extremely thin, and graceful. Her big, beautiful brown eyes and blond streaked hair color only added to her attractiveness. Her long, lean torso melted into legs that flowed into her designer shoes. She tried to get Declan's attention. He didn't appear to be affected by her at all. Unfortunately, *I* was affected by the looks she gave him and not in a good way.

Malevolence. That was the first word I thought of. She reminded me of the evil queen in *Sleeping Beauty*. The way she approached Declan told me that they had unfinished business.

If apprehension was a weapon, then I needed to stockpile my arsenal. As I watched her, I knew that I couldn't trust this woman. I didn't know what, how, or why, but my senses were warning me with red, flashing lights in my head. I knew that she meant trouble and I was on high alert. I was filled with protective feelings for Declan. This woman meant him serious harm.

My instincts told me that she had feelings for Declan. She

looked at him possessively. I felt uncomfortable about the shady aura that surrounded her. He had never mentioned his previous relationships to me and I wondered if she was one of the women he'd left behind. If that was the case, she looked like she wanted him to pay for it.

I shifted in my seat. I had never felt the need to protect Declan. Instead, I enjoyed feeling protected by him. He was in great shape physically, but I knew that this battle wouldn't require his strength. Some women play manipulative games and she looked like she had invented them. The closer she got to him, the wider her fake smile grew; when he did catch a glimpse of her, he dismissed her with a look of indifference. Her face immediately contorted. Like a beautiful monster, her look said that she didn't like or accept the belittlement. A knot formed and twisted in my stomach. Everything about her spelled trouble, but I was out of my element. I spent most of my time with carpenters, plumbers, and electricians; not lethal and gorgeous women. Although I told myself to relax, I couldn't. Mentally and physically, I postured for a wave to hit.

I didn't want to watch anymore of their silent sparring, so I tried to concentrate on my work. I was working on a surprise for Declan. As I sketched, I tried to put Declan's dream on paper. We'd spent countless hours talking about the business that he wanted to open on the Eastern Shore. I'd even gone so far as to ask Paige to find listings of commercial properties for sale. This could be more than his dream; it could be his reality. I'd pushed him to write everything down so that he would be one step closer to achieving his goal. He'd been talking about it for months, but hadn't taken any action. That was where he and I differed. When it came to business, I was a woman of action and, so far, he was all talk. I could only hope that my secret project would speed up the process.

As I tried to bury myself in concentration, the woman's voice distracted me. Although I couldn't make out the words, I detected the Latin accent. Her tone was sexy and condescending at the same time and Declan wasn't happy. As the photographers positioned them closer, she was too close for my comfort. Like the green-eyed monster it was reputed to be, jealousy ate my confidence in little bites. I looked at the other people on the set. *Was I the only one who could see the power play?*

I was flooded with unfamiliar feelings. My desire to protect him overrode my jealousy. Suddenly, I felt vicious. She was a snake. Her arms and legs slinked over him provocatively while she eyed him up like prey. He refused to play into it, which only made her more determined. Although he remained professional, an air of resistance and irritation clouded the room. If she exemplified the type of people he worked with, it was no wonder he couldn't wait to get away. As I processed the scene before me, I felt an urgency to help bring his vision to reality. As far as this bitch in front of me? I'd seen a lot of beautiful snakes while working construction. They didn't scare me.

I looked at my watch. Declan had told me that the theatre was booked for several hours and that time was almost done. He'd made eye contact with me through some of the poses and I returned his glance with comforting smiles. He was so handsome. My heart quickened when he winked at me and I blew him a kiss. The gestures were subtle, but the woman noticed the direction of his gaze. She channeled a few looks of her own toward me. None of them were pleasant.

I didn't want him to stress over me, so I kept my eyes down for the most part, giving an indifferent appearance. To him it looked like I was doing exactly what I said I would be, but my senses were on high alert. I caught a few of the words that she exchanged with him because since she was aware of me, she raised her voice. I remained professional, although my mind was muddled. I didn't want to distract him from his work, but I was counting the minutes until he was done. Finally, the photographer's voice echoed and thanked everyone for their work. A sigh of relief escaped me. I was happy to be getting out of there. I couldn't wait to go back to the apartment where it would be just the two of us.

As I gathered my things, he walked toward me. The woman was still on the stage speaking with the photographer. Declan's footsteps made a scraping sound against the floor as he walked down the aisle toward my seat. His arm came around my waist and he kissed me.

"I'll only be a few minutes. I have to get my stuff from backstage."

"I'll be ready when you come back out." He towered over me. Up close, I could see the final product of the makeup artist and hairstylist. His face had a matte finish on top of his tanned skin and his hair was stiff with spray. I wrinkled up my nose. "Are we going back to the apartment before we go out?"

He laughed. "So I can get all this shit off of me? Yeah." He pulled me close and whispered in my ear. "Maybe we can pick up where we left off in the shower."

I felt the heated blush flood my cheeks as he released me. I nodded toward the stage.

"Who is she?"

He didn't look in that direction; instead, he kept his attention on me. "Her name's Marisol." He squeezed my hand. "I'll be right back."

I watched as Declan disappeared behind the stage.

Marisol.

Definitely a name I wouldn't forget.

CHAPTER
Twenty-Three

Declan

I couldn't wait to get the hell out of here. Marisol had been a bitch all morning. I saw her look over at Aria several times. Knowing her reputation for creating a scene, I didn't want Aria exposed to her or her temper tantrums. At the completion of the shoot, I immediately walked toward Aria, choosing to delay my normal routine of removing the heavy makeup. From the corner of my eye, I saw Marisol talking to the photographer, so I took advantage of the opportunity to grab my stuff, get Aria, and leave. Unfortunately, she intercepted me as I approached the backstage area. Aria was in direct view of the exchange.

"Declan. I've missed you." Her purred, heavy accent grated on my ears. "It's been too long. You ran away the last time we were together." She placed a pointed fingernail onto my chest. Her tone suggested a familiarity that didn't exist. I was sure the show was for Aria's benefit. "You were a *very bad boy.*" She spoke in staccato as she tapped her finger with each of the last three words. "That wasn't very nice," she chastised.

I looked her straight in the eye, my message clear by my tone. "What I did, and what I do, is none of your business."

She became indignant. She didn't take kindly to defiance or being put in her place. A flame of bitterness lit in her eyes, yet she had complete control of her tone.

Placing a smile on her face, she moved closer. Her hand dropped from my chest to my leg and ran up my thigh. "You're such a bad boy, teasing me."

Before her fingers reached their intended destination, I gripped her wrist and squeezed. Hard. I spoke through gritted teeth. "You shouldn't touch what doesn't belong to you."

Her eyes narrowed as she turned her head toward Aria. The look Aria gave back was one I'd never seen. It should have sliced Marisol in two and made her back off, but it only antagonized her further. Marisol looked from Aria to me. With an icy smile, she looked between my eyes and her wrist.

"Baby, I know your games. All you had to do was ask." She licked her lips. "You know I like it when you play rough, lover," she said in a sexy voice, coming within inches of my face.

She was pissing me off with her game and I wasn't playing. I didn't care if I made a scene. I looked into her black eyes. My tone was purposely slow and succinct so that the meaning was crystal clear. "Get this straight. I've never played and never will. Got it?" I flung her wrist so hard it should have slapped her in the face.

I moved myself away and out of her reach. I was done with this charade. I'd put up with her only for publicity and right now I didn't give two shits if this encounter was broadcast in every rag magazine that existed. I couldn't work with her anymore. I was done. I was ready to call my agent and break my contract. No matter what it cost.

CHAPTER
Twenty-Four

Aria

I stayed composed, but wanted to break out into a monumental smile. Declan's expression was as hard as stone. The message had been delivered by his commanding presence. An aura of power surrounded him as he approached me.

"Ready?" The depth of his baritone rocked me. I sensed the anger that he was struggling to control. I nodded and grabbed my bag. He walked behind me as we neared the exit door.

"Shit!" He stopped and I turned. "I left my phone backstage." He dropped his bag to the floor. "Stay here. I'll be right back."

He jogged to the area where the crew was cleaning up. A strained hush had fallen over the staff that were witnesses to the scene between him and Marisol. He'd embarrassed her and the fury of that fact was still registered on her face. She turned her resentful stare toward me as the culprit behind her disgrace. We were instant enemies. Although I had no reason to get personal with her, by the look in her eyes, she was going to make it that way. She walked toward me.

"He is a most pretty man, is he not?" Her thick accent had a lethal sexuality about it. I steeled myself inside, refusing the intimidation.

"*Pretty* isn't a word I'd use to describe Declan." Sarcasm dripped in my tone.

"Perhaps you're right," she said as she closed the distance between us. "There are better words to describe him." She stopped. A few aisles separated us, but I was blanketed by the evil that surrounded her. "*Thick ... hard ... big ...* Those are better words." She emphasized each one as she challenged me wearing a malevolent smile. "I don't believe we've met. I'm Marisol Franzi—a very ... *special* ... friend of Declan's."

I looked for him over her shoulder. I didn't want to be here. I wanted out. Away from her. I just wanted to go. Our plans were to have a nice dinner and do some "touristy" things in New York since it was new to me. She'd built a wall of confrontation in those few minutes and I wasn't mentally prepared. *Where was he?* As I continued to look over her shoulder, she continued.

"You do know that we're involved, right? That I'm his girlfriend?"

Shock washed over me in an unexpected wave. My eyes went right to hers. There was no sincerity in them. She was lying and she was using him to shake me.

My shoulders straightened as my body grew stiff. "If you were important to *him*, I would have introduced myself. Obviously, he doesn't share your delusion or he would have mentioned you." She narrowed her eyes as boldness burst inside me. "I know Declan to be an *excellent* judge of character, so I'll follow his lead. Since he didn't mention you, you must be insignificant. As for you being Declan's girlfriend? That would never happen except in your delusional mind."

Out of the corner of my eye, I saw Declan. A look of shock came over him when he realized what was happening. Though my knees were shaking, I refused to let her see. As he made his way toward me, I took a few steps in his direction. Marisol and I were near-ly shoulder-to-shoulder as a threat fell from my lips.

"Leave him alone and get the hell out of my way." I looked into her eyes, but still kept him in sight.

A vicious veil fell over her perfect features. "Who the *hell* do you think you are, you little puta bitch! Why you're nothing but a—"

A hand of steel gripped her upper arm, spinning her around.

"Enough!"

CHAPTER
Twenty-Five

Aria

H e was still holding onto her as he looked at me. Concern was all over his face.

"Aria?"

I nodded, assuring him that I was okay. If I used words, they might have betrayed my emotions. Although I had stood up to her, I was shaking inside. He turned to Marisol with a cold stare. His voice pummeled her look of defiance.

"I don't know what poison you're spilling, but it stops. Now! Crawl back into your hole!" She stumbled as he released her.

He gripped my hand, looking into my eyes to assure himself that I was okay. One second later, he was leading me out of the theatre. The sound of Marisol's voice filled the empty space.

"I didn't know you wanted to keep us a secret. Don't be mad. I'll make it up to you."

We could still hear her raised voice as the door closed behind us. His expression had escalated from anger to rage. Even though I knew that I wasn't the cause, it was a look that I didn't want to see again.

He pulled me into the waiting limo. I left him alone with his thoughts for several minutes as I looked out the window. I didn't say anything until I realized that we were leaving the city.

"Where are we going?"

"Home."

"Home? Why aren't we going back to the apartment?"

"Because I don't want to. We're going home." His anger collided with my confusion. Now I was angry. He was the one that had convinced me to come on this trip. Telling me how great it would be if I were with him. Promising to show me the city. Now all that had changed because of *her*? My nerves were pushed to the edge.

"No, Declan! I don't know what the hell that was back there, but I'm not going to suffer for it. You're the one who painted the pretty picture of this trip and now you're letting another woman ruin it. And you're acting like you're mad at me. Who is she? Some crazy, bitchy, ex-girlfriend?" I was fuming.

"You don't know what the hell you're talking about. She's never been my girlfriend. That's just something the press made up. Don't be stupid."

What the hell? Now I'm stupid?

"Screw you! You're not talking to me like this. I don't know what buttons she pushed, but this is not *my* issue. Take your misdirected anger and shove it up your ass! Better yet, shove it up *hers!*"

I moved away from him.

"Oh no, you don't!" He took my hand and tried to pull me close, but I was so filled with anger that I shoved him back. I only looked at him long enough to see the mixture of anger and passion in his eyes.

"Get off of me! You're being an ass!" I wasn't playing this game.

"No." He succeeded in getting close by pulling me at my waist. He took my chin in his hand and made me look into his eyes. "I'm not letting Marisol and her mind games get between us! This is *exactly* what she wants!"

He held the back of my head and crushed his lips to mine. I

struggled, but he wouldn't release me. Our emotions exploded until neither of us could think or breathe.

He let go and stared into my eyes. I was infuriated and excited, but he was right. Marisol was toxic and we'd let her come between us.

"It stops." His words were soft. "Please."

The look in his eyes melted my indignation. He took my mouth again, but this time it was all passion. His touch was sincere as he held me.

"I want to go *home*, Aria. You and me. I used to think that the beach was magic, but it's not the beach. It's you."

I was sure that he could hear my heart as the beats sped up and I swallowed the lump in my throat. This was the Declan that I knew. His emotions stripped and bare. Telling me that home wasn't a place. It was me.

My anger abated, I knew exactly what he needed.

He needed to go home.

CHAPTER
Twenty-Six

Declan

I always looked forward to the Fourth of July. My memories of spending Independence Day at the beach were filled with Fisher's popcorn, Thrasher's fries, and fireworks over the ocean. I was hoping to make some new memories with Aria, but for her, this celebration would be bittersweet. It was the first one without her dad.

We'd been together for nearly a year and as the days went by, we began to fit together like a puzzle. As with all new things, especially living arrangements, adjustments were made. Our twenty-four hour personalities had become better acquainted. When she irritated me, I exercised tolerance. When I drove her crazy, she learned to speak up. We challenged each other in many ways. I got her to try new things because she'd lived a more sheltered life than I had. They were little things like ordering something new in restaurants or driving to places she'd never been before for an afternoon hike and picnic. Her delight became *my* delight. Her emotions were always transparent. It was one of the things I loved most about her. She wasn't fake. I'd learned to read her expressions and today I saw strain. I tempted her with the smell of freshly made coffee. If anything could entice her to come downstairs, that could. I smiled to myself when she walked into the kitchen.

"Hey beautiful. Want some coffee?"

"Yes, please." She laid her head down on her arms.

I poured a cup and placed it in front of her. When she didn't budge, I pulled my chair over. As I brushed the hair from her face, I saw trouble brewing in her eyes.

"Talk to me. What's wrong, baby?"

Struggling between tears and words, it took a few moments until she leaned up on her elbow. When she did, she shrugged her shoulders.

"I'm excited for tonight—for you to meet the family." She glanced in my direction. "Really, I am. And I can't wait to watch the fireworks with everybody, especially you. Mom loves you and I'm excited for you to meet my aunts, uncles, and cousins, and all the little ones. They're going to love you, too. I know it's going to be great."

Her words grew slower and sadder and she tried to hide her tears, so I pushed. "But?"

She turned up her chin. Tears trickled down as her voice began to tremble. "But ... Dad's not here."

I put my hand over hers and nodded understanding.

"Don't get me wrong. It's going to be fun. My aunts are going to gush all over you and Uncle Bill's wife, Thelma, is going to make you eat until you're stuffed. Seriously. She's so hospitable that you'll feel like you've known her forever. Everybody will be talking and laughing, but when everyone goes out on the front porch ..."

Her voice trailed off as more tears began to fall. "Tell me. What's making you cry?"

"It's the porch," she confessed. "My dad was sick for a long time. His legs always hurt him. But he never stopped going on vacation. Sitting on the porch was his favorite part." She looked up at me. "You know those chairs? The big green Adirondacks? He commandeered one of them. Made it *his* chair. He was there for coffee in the morning and a beer at night. There were many conversations on that porch. He was like a king on a throne as everybody went out there to talk to him. Everybody. They knew he couldn't go up and down all of the steps because of his legs, so they came to him. He was in his element. Relaxing and talking. Bullshitting and solving all the world's problems. He laughed about the old days, arguing politics ... but in that chair? He was happy." She chuckled. "Even though it wasn't really *his* chair, you know?"

I squeezed her hand.

"On each Fourth of July, for just *that* night, he forgot his pain. Even though it was an act; it was like he wasn't as sick as we knew he was. I remember him smiling, laughing ... just one of the guys. Declan ... I'm almost afraid to go. Just thinking about being there without him ... I don't want to be like this in front of everybody. I just feel torn. I want to go because I want you to meet everybody, but I don't want to go because he isn't there."

My sweet girl was breaking my heart. I wanted to make the pain go away, but I knew she needed to work this out on her own. She would. Although she couldn't see it, she was one of the strongest people I knew. I pulled her onto my lap and held her close for a few minutes, then I brushed the long strands away from her face.

"I get it. I want to meet them all too, but if you're putting your-self through this for me, we can wait till it's easier. Maybe next year."

She shook her head. "No. I want to go. I have to do it." She managed a weak smile. "No time like the present, right?"

"Look at it this way. You'll be so busy introducing me to every-one that you won't even have time to feel sad. Didn't you say there's, like, a million of them?"

She laughed. "No, not a million; just a few hundred or so."

"You just introduce me and I'll turn on my Madison Avenue charm. Remember, your mom's going to be there too. Tonight's go-ing to be hard on her as well, but if your family is the way you de-scribe everybody will be so busy talking and laughing that you and your mom will be okay."

She nodded again, but looked hesitant.

"The hard part is going to be after dinner, right? On the porch?"

"Yeah," she whispered.

"I'm going to be right there with you, baby. Right by your side. I won't leave you. Promise. You don't have to do this by yourself, okay?"

"But what about after the fireworks? When everyone goes back and hangs out there for hours?

"We don't have to stay, Aria. When it's over, we'll walk back to our place, just you and me. You can tell your mom before we go up for the fireworks. I'm sure she'll understand. Sound like a plan?"

Her body relaxed as she decompressed in my arms and rested her head on my shoulder. I felt complete when I was helping to solve her problems or protecting her.

"Thank you." I felt her head snuggle into my shoulder.

"For what?"

"For taking care of the little things. I love you for that."

Warmth stirred in my chest. With Aria, it was always about the little things. "Baby, never thank me for that. I love you. You'd do the same for me."

CHAPTER
Twenty-Seven

Declan

It hadn't taken long for Aria to get ready. It had taken more time to walk from my house to *The Skipjack*. The streets and the boardwalk were filled with thousands of people. Fourth of July at the beach was the busiest time of the season. People flocked to all of the seaside resorts and Ocean City was no exception.

Aria had not exaggerated. Her family was huge. By the time she had taken me around for introductions, a few hours had passed. I picked up toddlers, held babies, and got kisses and handshakes from aunts, uncles, and cousins. This was completely foreign to me, as it had always been just Carter, my mom, and me.

When we gathered for dinner, Aria's Aunt Thelma made sure that I'd had at least a taste of every dish prepared. They were delicious. Every one of them. There was a flurry of activity as everyone pitched in to clean up and I offered my services. Aria told me that I didn't need to help, but I teased her by saying that if I didn't work out regularly, her family's cooking would put me out of a job. And they weren't just generous with food. Each person went out of their way to make me feel as if they had known me for years.

The crowd had thinned out now that dinner was over. A few of her aunts were still in the kitchen, but she hadn't made a move from the table. I could see in her expression that she was mentally bracing herself to step out onto the porch.

"You know, I also have memories of that porch."

She cocked an eyebrow.

"I remember counting the steps when we went out for the first time and I remember the first time I kissed you."

"I know. I'm avoiding."

I squeezed her hand.

She pushed her chair away from the table. "Let's go."

We walked through the rooms until we reached the screen door. Aria swallowed as she placed her hand against the freshly painted wood. It creaked as she pushed through. Her sad eyes went to the large, green Adirondack all the way on the left. She took some deep breaths as she stared at the chair. No one else noticed, but I was paying attention. The door opened and closed behind us and I heard footsteps. Aria reacted. Something was different. She was still shaky, but her apprehension was gone. She was smiling.

"Are you okay?" I placed my arms around her waist and pulled her back to my chest.

"Surprisingly, yes." She lifted her chin. "It's Uncle Bill. He switched," she whispered. "He knows ... and he's dad's best friend."

At first I didn't get it, but she nodded toward the chair. Uncle Bill's attention was on Aria. He winked at her. He was sitting in her dad's chair instead of the one he normally occupied. As I tightened my hold, Uncle Bill looked at me with approval. I felt a sense of satisfaction by that simple gesture. For me, it was the next best thing to getting her father's blessing.

Her neck relaxed and she molded against me. I tilted my head so that I could see her expression. Aria was smiling.

True to Aria's recollections, the children were allowed to go ahead of the adults. They all knew their designated boundaries. Some of the family brought chairs, while others had blankets.

The sky darkened as the time drew near for the fireworks display. By then, most of the family were on the beach. We shared a blanket away from the crowd for a little space and privacy. She arranged the corners to her satisfaction then sat down between my bent knees. I pulled her against me. She'd been quiet during the walk up to the beach. I kissed her head.

"How you doing, beautiful?"

"Better than I thought I'd be."

She pulled her hair to one side. A warm breeze played with the strands. She slowly ran her fingers through the long curls to ward off tangles.

"I'm glad you were with me today. I was afraid it was going to be terribly sad. Having you there made it easier," she said quietly.

"How about the porch? How was that?"

"Truth?" She paused, then let out a sigh. "I'm exhausted. I knew *someone* was going to sit there. I almost cried when I saw that it was Uncle Bill. Not because I was sad, but because I was happy that it was him rather than someone else. If it had been anybody else ..." She leaned up and rolled her head from side to side to ease the tension in her neck. "It's funny, you know? You don't think about stuff like this when you're a kid. Things are just the way they are and you expect them to always stay that way." Her voice trembled with emotion. "When Daddy felt pain, *real* pain, he never complained. I spent many a morning having coffee with him out there and then he got really sick. That's when I started bringing *him* coffee. He'd lost so much weight and muscle by then that he also needed pillows. But he never gave up that spot. Seeing Uncle Bill in Dad's chair was okay." She paused again and then whispered, "Thank you. I'm good. And you helped."

She relaxed against my chest. As the fireworks lit up the sky, I wrapped my arms around my sweet, beautiful girl. I placed my lips against her ear to ensure that she could hear me above the cracks and booms.

"I'll always be here for you. I love you."

She looked up and into my eyes. Hers were moist with unshed tears.

"I love you too, Bear. With all my heart."

CHAPTER
Twenty-Eight

Marisol

Marisol reclined on the penthouse balcony, barely noticing the illumination filling the sky. Her mood was as dark as the night. She had seen enough. At least the investigator's information had been correct. Declan was exactly where he said he would be. Why he seemed so relaxed with that little bitch was beyond her comprehension. They barely knew each other! She and Declan had worked together for years. He had never acted like that with her. And the way he had dismissed her after the photo shoot? The little bitch would pay.

CHAPTER
Twenty-Nine

Aria

I stood with my friend, Paige Kasey, in the middle of a building that formerly housed a gym. It was on a large corner lot at a major intersection on Coastal Highway. She had found the perfect building and location. The building had just come up on the market. Paige was the listing realtor, so she was giving me a great opportunity to realize the first step in Declan's dream.

This building was exactly what he'd described to me. He had laid out every detail of his vision until I saw it in my mind's eye. The only problem was that he was away on business in Tokyo and wouldn't be returning for another two days. I wasn't sure that the space would last that long once she put it on the market. I had mentioned what I was looking for when we'd had lunch a few months ago. She said she'd keep her eye out. And here we were.

"At first glance, it looks like it needs a lot of work, but it does look like a great spot for a photo studio. A good name with proper signage would pique interest. It's a cool, geometric design that would attract a lot of young people. Exactly what he said he wanted. What do you think?"

I could trust Paige to be totally honest. She wasn't a realtor who'd just throw a sales pitch together for the commission. It wasn't her style. She took her time with her clients and got a great deal of satisfaction by matching the right buyer with the right property. And she was my best friend.

We had met at the beach when we were kids and reunited in college. It was during that time that she developed an interest in aesthetics. She was a girl that was into appearances and real estate could be transformed. She found the fixer-uppers and with good tradesmen and a little money, she turned them for a profit. I was her hairstylist. I worked part-time while in college, specializing in wigs and hairpieces. While I created hairstyles out of nothing, she added properties to her portfolio and money to her bank account. Although the work I did was rewarding, it took a heavy personal toll. I was very sensitive and felt the pain of my clients, sometimes to the point where I didn't want to get out of bed. Paige convinced me that my artist's eye had other uses and suggested remodeling when the hair business got to be too much for me. She knew that I was my father's understudy and loved the work we'd done together. Paige's business had a reputation for integrity and it was less than ten years old. She was well on her way to becoming a multi-millionaire.

"Declan said he needs a lot of room for the photography side, but space to conduct meetings as well. That would include a work area for support staff." My voice echoed as I looked over the space. "You know what's on the market. I want your professional opinion."

She looked around at the square footage. It couldn't be called a room because it was a big, empty shell.

"I think it has fantastic potential. The ceilings are high, so he could adjust the lighting however he'd like. Same goes with setting up the structure, seeing as there are no interior walls to remove. For studio space, it looks good to me, but only Declan would know the specifics of what he's looking for."

"Let me try to call him." I took the leather bag from my shoulder and dug through it for my cell.

"You go ahead. I'm going to look around some more in case he doesn't want it. I have a few clients in mind."

The click of her high heels decreased as I walked to the outside of the building to call Declan. "Please pick up. Please pick up," I said to myself. I got his voicemail.

"You've reached Declan Sinclair. You know what to do."

Damn! I really needed to talk to him. Frustrated, I left a message.

"Hey babe. *Please* call me when you get this message. I have something exciting to tell you. Talk to you soon."

I disconnected the call and walked back into the building. Paige was leaning against the wall looking at her cell.

"Tell me the truth. Once this goes on the market, how long do you think it'll last?"

"Honestly, I don't think it is going to last a day."

I felt the shock register on my face. *A day?* "You have to be kidding!" She put up her hand in an effort to silence me.

"I know, but let me play out a scenario for you, Aria." She twirled and waved her arms around the big room. "This huge box is a blank canvas of a building. Although most of the revenue in this town comes during the summer months, resort areas are gradually moving toward becoming four-season places to escape. You've been here through the seasons. Haven't you noticed how many businesses are open on the weekends?"

I shrugged my shoulders. Had I ever paid attention?

"Oh, come on. You *must* have noticed. Haven't you seen people walking on the beach, even in the dead of winter? A lot of people are moving here, from retirees to those that want a retreat. This would make a great building for condos and lots of investors are more than willing to cater to the market."

She had a point. I could see where she was going with this and I knew that she was right.

"I guess I have noticed."

"Sure you have," she mocked. "You only have eyes for Declan." She rolled her eyes and we both laughed. "Seriously, real estate is at its prime here, especially commercial real estate. Look at what we're standing in! Can *you* see the possibilities? Paige was making her case.

"I don't know what to do. What if I can't reach him? I know what his business plan is. He's shared it with me many times, but this is a big step. I don't want to presume what he wants, but I don't want him to lose it."

Paige just smiled and cocked her head at me. "I can't tell you what to do, but you've heard it before. There's no time like the present."

"Let me go outside and try to call him one more time."

As I exited the building, I punched his number into the keypad for the fifth time and again got his voicemail. *Ugh!* "Please call me as soon as you get this."

Then I had an epiphany. My brain went into overdrive and I began to pace. Deep in thought, but terrified, a plan began to form. Declan had said that he was just waiting for the *right* property and the *right* opportunity to come along. *This was it!*

I walked out the door and a bit further away away from the building for a better perspective. Huge building. Great location. Right price. *Yes! This was it!*

The one thing I'd always been blessed with was vision. As I went back inside, I imagined the entire project completed. In my mind's eye, I saw a beautiful studio space with more than enough room for make-up artists, hair stylists, dressers, and photographers. There was ample space for the state-of-the-art studio that he had envisioned with plenty of natural light for the photographers and adequate office and meeting space. People would be crazy not to partner with him.

My mind raced. He had said this town was where he wanted to start his business. I teetered on the edge of fear and decision when I heard Paige's footsteps approach. She took me by the hand and led me to one side of the building.

"There's one more thing that we didn't consider. Look at this view! Adding a second floor would give you the bay view. That's a better landscape than any painting you could hang on the wall."

It was a *spectacular* view. At every turn there was confirmation that this building was perfect. *If I could just contact him!*

"Paige, I'd like to bring my inspector by to check it out. Do you think the price is negotiable?"

"Are you serious? They'll expect a contingency contract. The price is that good."

"Let's put in an offer."

CHAPTER
Thirty

Declan

"You did what?!" I couldn't believe the words. Aria was on the phone and I was certain we had a terrible connection.

"I bought a building. For you."

Even though she'd repeated herself, I was still in shock. The silence was deafening for the next few minutes and then I began to ramble.

"Why in God's name would you buy a building for *me*?! Without me? Are you out of your mind?! A *building*?" The incredible disbelief continued to register in my voice.

"Declan, calm down; it's only a building. You can look at it when you get back. It was the perfect size for the studio you described and time was of the essence." She paused. "I did try to reach you."

"Calm down? It's *only* a building? You tried to reach me?"

"Stop repeating me."

"Really? There's a thirteen-hour time difference, Aria. I was sleeping. That's why I didn't answer the phone. I have another day of work here; we're shooting at Tokyo Tower. How in the hell am I supposed to concentrate when you've bought a building?!"

"Oh for God's sake!" The exasperation in her voice traveled through the airwaves. "Seriously. You don't need to worry about anything. I do stuff like this all the time, remember? The paperwork's done. The ink is dry. You know Paige. She's a reputable businesswoman as well as my friend. She'd never sell me a property I couldn't flip. And she's always careful to dot every *i* and cross every *t*. I've worked with her since I started my business. Remember?"

"Yes, I do remember. That's beside the point. Why couldn't you wait for me to come home? We could have looked at it together."

"Honestly, there was no time. Paige had inside information that the owner was in financial straits. He was motivated to move quickly. Paige gave me a tour before it was listed because she is the agent. If I hadn't taken it, it would have been gone by the time you got back."

"Aria, you presume too much. How do you know the building is the amount of space that I want? Or that the space is even what would be needed for a studio? Can it accommodate more than one session at the same time?"

"Calm down …"

"You've been with me on what? Four, five shoots? You don't know what goes into a photo session; what particulars are needed for the photographers, assistants, and anybody else, for that matter. You have *no idea* what's required for my business."

Silence. Deafening silence and a thirteen-hour time difference. With the phone to my ear, all I could do was shake my head. Then she spoke slowly and succinctly. Her tone was indignant.

"What do you mean, I have *no idea* what specifications are required for *your* business? Exactly what are you trying to say?"

"I'm trying to say you should mind *your own* business. Not mine."

"Really, Declan? Well, since the possibility exists that I have no idea what goes into a business, then perhaps you'd like to enlighten me."

Suddenly she'd gone from benevolent angel to grim reaper. How dare she get pissed off at me! I didn't do anything! I caught my breath. My chest hurt from a brew of ugly emotions: exasperation, frustration, exhaustion, worry, and anxiety. A firestorm of a migraine pounded inside my head. In my gut I knew her intentions were good, but buying someone a building? *Who does that?* I tried to take my tone down a notch.

"What I'm trying to say is that I know your intentions were good, but you shouldn't have done it without me. You may have bitten off more than you could chew. Your dad isn't here to help you with this one. What do you know about commercial renovations?" The silence on the other end of the phone lasted so long, I thought we had been disconnected. "Hello?"

"You … think … my success in this business is because my dad was *with* me on the renovations? What, exactly, do you think he did? Hold my hand? Let's make something perfectly clear, *Mr. Sinclair*. I am an independent business owner. And I do excellent work. As a matter of fact, some of the best in my field. My daddy didn't hold my hand—he *empowered* me to perform my job. I *own* my company. I work damn hard. And I'm not afraid to take a chance, which is more than I can say for you. And if you were here, the *girlfriend* in me would slap your pretty face. You're insulting!"

"You don't have to act so pissed."

"As far as the *commercial* renovations on your project? Well, I don't know, *Mr. Sinclair*. Perhaps you should put out your feelers to get the names of some good contractors. Or look in the Yellow Pages. I don't care! Let's see how good you are at getting your project up and running without me, because up until sixty seconds ago, you had the best in the business. Your girlfriend is no longer interested in doing business with you, asshole! Because you wouldn't want someone who's afraid to work without holding her daddy's hand!"

"Look. I don't mean to say …"

"While you've been in Tokyo, a good—no, a *great*—building came on the market. It was perfect for a project you've been telling me about for a year. Great location. Great square footage. I, in what you believe to be my *limited* capabilities as a woman and an owner of my own company, saw an excellent opportunity for you! *You*, who have gone on *ad nauseam* about your hopes, dreams, and aspirations for your own business. And I had the balls to do something about it. Maybe you thought I wasn't listening to you droning on about what you *planned* to do—or maybe you didn't think that this *mere woman* could comprehend the complexity. Either way, you're an idiot."

She paused and I tried to interject. "But there's so much that has to be considered. Did you remember ..."

"Let's see what my little brain did remember, okay? Hmm ... in one day, *I* had inspectors—yes, inspectors, plural—inside the building to checkout the entire structure. Plumbing, electrical, insulation, and roofing. All of it! I had subcontractors—my subcontractors—come in and take estimated measurements so that they'd be prepared to sit down and intelligently speak with you about your specific design and aspirations for your dream to become a reality. I also spoke with a sign company—who respects and admires *my* reputation—anxious to work with you on whatever signage you want because of your relationship to me. So. I ask you—does it sound like *the little woman* just may have covered any concerns you might have had for *your* business?"

She stopped talking. Finally.

I didn't know what to say, so I said nothing. I could, however, hear her breathing—very hard—on the other end. There was no question that she was angry.

I backpedaled, hoping for damage control. "Aria ..."

"No, Declan don't. Just ... don't. You don't need to explain anything. I'm beginning to believe that what you've been describing to me is a dream, not a business. I think you like *the idea* of having your own business. You enjoy talking about it, writing ideas on paper, and even going so far as to have drawings made of how you would lay it out; but when opportunity smacks you in the face, you're scared. You're afraid of your own success. You're the one who needs someone to hold your hand and I would have been happy to do that, but you screwed it up."

I had nothing. I was tired and angry. I took offense to every word she'd just unleashed on me.

"Don't concern yourself. It is, after all, just a building. My name is on the contract, not yours. Regardless of the original intent with which I made the purchase, I'm confident I can turn a profit. *You* may be afraid of business, Declan, but *I'm* not."

This is bullshit! "Look, I know you're pissed off, but my concerns are valid and you know it. Your personal attacks aren't necessary."

"Declan, this has nothing to do with me being pissed off; it has *everything* to do with your confidence in me and my ability. So I'll say it again; *my* name is on the contract. You're under no obligation."

I could hear the hurt in her voice and my heart clenched. We had never fought like this. I would have preferred to have this conversation face-to-face.

"We can talk more about it when I get home. Then we can make a decision."

"Oh no, we won't! My mind's made up. I *know* it is a good investment. You may not trust me, but I trust myself; and you know what? I *do* have good instincts and they're telling me that I made the right decision. Screw your reservations."

A knock on the door interrupted the conversation and I absentmindedly answered it.

"Hello, lover. The car's waiting for us."

"I'll be right down." I closed the door on Marisol, hoping Aria hadn't recognized her voice.

No. Such. Luck.

"Perfect ... *just perfect.*"

"Look, I have to get ready for work. I don't want to hang up until we get this straightened out." My head was pounding. Aria's voice grew eerily cryptic.

"We can't always get what we want."

CHAPTER
Thirty-One

Declan

"Paige? This is Declan Sinclair. I spoke with Aria. She told me that the purchase of the building is underway. I want to see if I can cancel ..."

She interrupted me. I was attempting to keep my tone calm and my anger under control.

"Yes she did. But before you say anything, let me give you my professional opinion. I think the building's a great buy. I agree with her decision. It wouldn't have lasted long on the market. By the time I got back to the office with the contract, word had leaked that the building might be available. There is interest from three other parties. In my opinion, you got a great deal."

My anger deflated the moment she said three other parties. "It's that good, huh?"

"I think so."

I quickly mulled over a few thoughts. "Can I ask you to do me a favor?"

"That depends. I can cancel a contract. I won't hurt my friend."

"I'm not going to ask you to cancel the contract." I must be crazy. "I have a long flight back. Would it be possible for you to e-mail
some photos and a spec sheet on the building layout?"

"Sure, I can do that. Let me get a pen."

While she put me on hold, I began to think of the possibilities. I
could either get moving with my plans or start preparing my case to
justify why Aria shouldn't have done this. I was still incensed with
the thought that anyone would make that big of a decision for me.

"Declan, I think I have everything you need. I have photos of
both the inside and outside, day and evening shots, and architectural
drawings that were done before the building was a gym."

"That sounds great, Paige. Thanks—"

"Wait, that's not all," she interrupted.

"No?"

"I'm not sure if she would want me to send this, but I have a
rough copy of Aria's drawings. She was sketching the whole time
she was there and each time she got a new idea, she made a new
sketch. I held on to the ones she wanted to trash. I don't know if it
would help, but at least you could get an idea of how it could look.
Do you want me to send those as well?"

It sounded like Paige had everything I needed. Even though I
was doing this without Aria's knowledge, she was providing a
wealth of information and I could look everything over on the flight
home. I wanted to be completely prepared to justify to Aria that this
was a mistake that she should never repeat again and I wanted all my
points to be validated.

"Yes. Please send everything to me. And Paige?"

"Yes?"

"Will you be seeing Aria soon?"

"Yes. We're supposed to get together tomorrow."

"I'd appreciate it if you don't mention our conversation. I need
to look this over and do some mental preparation."

"Sure. I get it. Just know that you have three days to cancel."

"Okay. Thanks."

"Anything for a friend."

Why did that last remark make me feel like an enemy in a Trojan horse?

I slept on it. The migraine was a killer and I needed time to gain perspective. Sleep was exactly what I had needed and once I was done showering, I went down to the front desk. They had all of the information from Paige in a neat little package. Every piece of ammunition that I needed. It was seven at night in Ocean City and eight a.m. in Tokyo. I usually started my day much earlier, but there was little left on this job to do. I only had half a day of work ahead of me and I was hoping that it would end early.

As I looked over the paperwork, I got the sinking feeling that I had underestimated Aria. The space was amazing and was more than I needed. Her sketches were really good. It was becoming blatantly obvious that she had made the right decision. *Shit!* I hated to admit that she was right and I was wrong.

I hated being this far away from her and I hated when we fought. *And I hated Marisol for making matters worse.*

Most of my anger was because I was working with Marisol. She had become a thorn in my side and a pain in the ass. There was no metaphor to express how much I disliked her.

Before I met Aria, I was able to tolerate Marisol, but now her presence made me cringe. I tried not to react to her. I just wanted to get the job done and as long as she kept her mouth closed, we were fine. But she took too many liberties. Her hands roamed too freely and her fingers lingered too long. Her remarks were consistently suggestive and regardless of my public comments about my relationship with Aria, the woman would not leave me alone.

As I scanned the documents, I knew that when I saw Aria I would be eating my words.

CHAPTER
Thirty-Two

Declan

"**D**eclan, please stand over here. Marisol, I want you right here."

While the photographer, Jonatan, gave us direction, I was preoccupied with my thoughts. I had no more excuses. After further reviewing the package from Paige, I realized that Aria was right. About everything.

Part of me was excited about the idea of having my own business; however, when reality smacked me in the face, I did feel fear. It was a huge undertaking to make this dream of mine a reality. And I knew that I had hurt her. Insinuating that her business was successful because of her father's part in it was hurtful and insulting. *But it was partially true.* Aria did have someone by her side that she was able to trust for advice when she had started up her company. I'd never had someone I could trust like that. *Until now.*

My brother would listen to anything and everything I had to say, but he knew absolutely nothing about what I did. He thought I just stood in front of a camera. He didn't understand marketing and branding. He said that I was *overpaid for my pretty looks.* There were a handful of people that I'd hoped would work with me once the studio was up and running, but I needed to take that first step. Someone had to push me. Someone I could trust, confide in, and depend on.

Aria.

Knowing that I had not only pissed her off royally, but also had hurt and insulted her was distracting me.

"C'mon Dec. Get your head in the game so we can all go home."

Jonatan was right. We all wanted to go home, so I tried to clear my head and concentrate on work. For this particular photo, Marisol was supposed to look as if she was whispering something sexy in my ear. Both wrists were crossed, one over the other, and she was pressing into me. Even though music played, I could hear her voice clearly.

"What's wrong, lover? Little puta finally get on your last nerve?"

Her malicious tone baited me. She wanted to get a reaction and I wouldn't disappoint. I turned toward her, tilting my head slightly to give Jonatan a better shot. I looked straight into her eyes with a pose that would make the clients millions.

"I don't know what you're talking about. *You're* the only puta that gets on my last nerve."

I turned away from her and waited for Jonatan's next directive.

Surprisingly, Marisol kept it together well enough for the session to wrap up early. That should have been my first clue that she had an ulterior motive.

I had excused myself and returned to my room to look at the papers in further detail. The photos were awesome and the details of her design were great. If I moved ahead with this plan, I knew I wouldn't regret it. But I did regret discounting Aria. It was obvious that she'd listened to every detail. The sketches really got my attention. She had captured every thought I had. Her attention to detail was incredible. I felt like an ass. At least she loved me. I would have to explain to her how overwhelmed I had felt when she told me what she'd done. I sat back in the chair and closed the laptop. I needed a drink to help figure out how to fix this.

"Yes, Mr. Harris. It sounds exactly like what I'm looking for. Yes. A deep red. Garnet's her favorite. Uh huh. Thank you. Just send the information to my e-mail. I'll send confirmation. Yep. Thanks again."

I'd just bought my way out of the dog house by way of a phone call to Michael Harris, a business associate who lived on the Eastern Shore. I ate some food to clear my head and now I was relaxing and enjoying my drink. I felt good about what I'd just done. Aria would love it.

"Why do you dislike me so?"

I opened my eyes and saw Marisol sitting across from me.

"I neither like nor dislike you. I don't think of you. I merely work with you." My smile hid my irritation. She placed her elbow on the table and rested her chin in her hand. She could bat her eyelashes all she wanted. Her sex kitten act didn't work on me.

"You used to like me so much, but now that you are with that little girl, you never go to parties or shows ... no one ever sees us together anymore. It makes me sad—"

"Marisol, no one sees *us* together anymore because there was never an 'us' for anyone to see. We shared space at the same events because we worked together. Why can't you get that through your head?"

"No, lover. It was more than that. You liked me. They took our pictures. I cut out those pictures for my book. I saw the look on your face. You were happy with me. I know you wanted to have sex with me the night of that party ... and I know you were disappointed that it didn't happen."

She placed her hand on my arm and began rubbing up and down. She was pissing me off and ruining my mood. I gave her a look of disgust, but she continued.

"I'm the best, baby. These lips were made for sucking and this tongue was made for licking."

Like a snake, her tongue slid out. Slowly, she glided it over her top and bottom lips.

"I've seen you, Declan. I know how big you are. I would take you all night long … any way you want. Isn't that a better offer than playing in a sandbox?"

She was cunning and nasty. I leaned into her face, speaking slowly and deliberately. "Marisol, *baby*. Listen closely. We were never a *we*. Tabloids spun it that way to make money. That's all. As far as how I want you? How about the hell out of my sight?" I pushed out of my chair and left.

CHAPTER
Thirty-Three

Declan

"Carter, I screwed up."

It had been awhile since I'd talked to my brother, but I could always count on his honesty. He told me the truth, no matter how painful.

"Yeah. If you care that much, you've gotta decide what you're going to do about it. There's no middle ground here." Carter was right. He was always right.

"You know; I've never seen you so twisted-up over a woman before. You've never let anybody get that close. I guess that's a good thing."

My brother had hit the nail on the head. This "thing" with Aria wasn't a "thing" at all. It was more—so much more. Carter knew that. He was the only person that really knew me.

"Groveling and gifts are always good." He laughed into the phone.

"Yeah, I've already thought of that. Still, I wish she would have waited."

"She said she tried to call you. Are you going to keep beating that dead horse?" I heard my sister-in-law talking in the background.

"Okay, guys, enough. We need FaceTime."

It only took a minute and we were connected. It was good to see my family. I didn't know why we didn't FaceTime more often. They were all cozy. Lacey was sitting half on Carter's lap, half on the sofa, and he had his arm draped around her. I saw their beautiful Bernese Mountain Dog, Cody, lying near their feet.

"Hi, sweetie." Lacey took over the conversation. "I know you don't have much time, so I'm going to make this brief. *You* have to make this right. I heard everything that you said to Carter. I know all about the building for your studio, how Aria bought it, and how she should have waited for you, yadda, yadda, yadda ..." She waved her hands in the air. "What you need to know is this—she did it because she *loves* you. No woman—and I mean *no woman*—would ever put that much on the line for someone she didn't care about. *You* are behaving like a little school boy. I should know; I teach enough of them. I know how I'd feel if I was Aria—hurt and insulted. She stuck her neck out on the line for you. It most likely took her far out of her comfort zone. When you reacted the way you did ... you hurt her."

She moved off of Carter's lap and all I could see was Lacey's determined expression.

"Now, on a business level? That's an entirely different matter. Think of how you would have felt to hear the words you said. You completely devalued her as a businesswoman. You underestimated her. You say you love her? Well, love means trust. You would have given a realtor that you don't even know more consideration than you gave Aria. When you first started dating her, I looked her up on the internet. Have you seen her work? It's incredible! That woman is gifted. She's taken crap and made them palaces. And that comment about her dad? Do you see how childish and selfish that sounded?"

She wasn't saying anything that I didn't know. "Yes."

"What I'm saying, Dec, is that you screwed up. We all do it. So does Aria. Carter's right about groveling and gifts, but it's about so much more than that. She took a big chance, and she took it for you.

You're right; her business is in residential. She probably put up most of what she's invested in her own business for you to have a chance at yours."

Every word Lacey said was true. I remembered my mom saying *women think with their hearts and men with their heads.*

"You're right, Lacey ... and I'm an ass."

Carter and Lacey both laughed.

"Yes you are, baby brother!" Cody barked in agreement and ran around in circles. "Now enough with this FaceTime. Nothing beats the real thing, so when you get back to the beach and work this out with Aria—and you'd *better* work this out with her—come up here for a long weekend. We want to meet her in person."

"I second that!" Carter chimed in.

I promised that I'd do everything possible to work it out. I also promised to do as Lacey ordered and bring Aria to the mountains. She'd love the lake. After a few more minutes, we said our good-byes. I slipped my cell in my pocket. I had a long flight ahead of me, but I needed the time to carry out my plan. Aria would forgive me. She'd have to. I sent her a text.

Declan: *Sorry isn't enough, but I am.*

Aria: *They're just words.*

Declan: *I'm not a man for words, but I am sorry.*

Aria: ...

Declan: *I'm on my way home. I've set something up for you and your friends at the spa. When I get home, I'm taking you to dinner.*

Aria: *I don't know ...*

Declan: *Please ... :)*

Aria: *:) Ur nuts, you know that?*

Declan: *Only for you, baby. ;)*

Aria: *Ur not off the hook. We need to talk.*

Declan: :(

Aria: *The spa sounds nice. :)*

Declan: *It's all arranged. Just take the girls.*

Aria: *We still need to talk.*

Declan: *We can talk at dinner.*

Aria: *Ok ...*

Declan: *Love you.*

Aria: *Love you too ... but u still aren't off the hook.*

Declan: *You can punish me however you see fit. *wink, wink**

Aria: ;)

The plane was ready for takeoff. Now, if I could just get Mike Harris and my assistant, Katherine, on the phone, I could put the plan in motion.

CHAPTER
Thirty-Four

Aria

"Was that him?"

"Yes." I had gone to my mom's for dinner. My feelings and ego were still battered and bruised. Although his text seemed sincere, that type of hurt didn't just disappear for me.

"Put yourself in his place. When you first made the change from hairstyling to renovations, you had the support of Dad and me. You had your own finances, but you had the two of us as your cheerleaders. He doesn't have anyone cheering for him except you. His brother and sister-in-law wish him well, I'm sure, but it isn't the same as what Dad and I did for you. We were there every day. You bounced ideas off of us. We gave you our opinions, good and bad.

"But he has me and I'd help him, just like you and Dad helped me."

"It isn't the same, honey. Men want to take responsibility for their work. They want to achieve on their own."

"Sorry, but that just sounds like a load of crap. If I *can* help, I *want* to help. Because I love him. If he can't accept that because of some stupid macho bull, then …"

"All I'm saying is to give the man a chance. You love him and he loves you. He deserves a chance to explain."

"He sent me a text."

"At least he's communicating."

"He's sending me and the girls to the spa."

"Sounds like he's already trying to to rectify the situation."

My mom was pretty intuitive. I agreed that Declan should to have an opportunity to explain himself. Beyond that? We would see.

"To Men! You can't live with them; you can't live without them."

Paige raised her glass of wine and winked at me. "And they make it a little easier when they send you out for a day like this."

Everyone laughed.

I had built a small, but close, circle of friends in the past year. Aimee was a good friend of Declan's. Though they worked together, the two of us had become very close. She also lived at the beach part-time, but in Bethany, not Ocean City. She was a model and drop-dead gorgeous. The only other model I'd met was Marisol and she and Aimee were as different as night and day. Declan's assistant, Katherine, was a real sweetheart. She handled everything for him. I had introduced both girls to Paige and the four of us got together whenever we could.

"So what did Declan do?" Aimee's prying inquisitiveness was highlighted by a smile and rolling eyes. "He didn't send you to the spa for no reason."

"Nothing. He was just feeling generous," I lied.

"Sure and I'm the Duchess of Cambridge!" She smirked at me, then turned to Katherine. "C'mon. You're his assistant. I'm sure you know what crime he committed."

Katherine gave her an innocent look. "I have no idea, but I'm not going to look a gift horse in the mouth."

"I've known him a long time, and I've never known him to do this for any woman. He had to have done something."

Not swayed by insistence or interrogation, Katherine laid her head back against the pedicure throne and closed her eyes. "I don't know and I don't care. Even if I did, haven't you ever heard of a Confidentiality Agreement? You know I signed one of those when I started working for him."

Aimee flicked water at Katherine with her foot. Keeping her head back, Katherine popped open one eye. "Stop looking at me like that. I don't know any more than you do."

Paige took another sip of wine. "Well, I don't care what he did or didn't do and I think you should stop badgering the poor girl."

Aimee threw a little pillow at Paige, which barely missed falling in the footbath. "You know I'm just teasing! I love you, Aria." She blew me a kiss.

"Yes, I do. Not all supermodels hate me."

Aimee stopped laughing, her tone growing more serious. "This doesn't have anything to do with Marisol, does it?"

"Oh my gosh, no." I gave her a puzzled look. "Should it?" Immediately, I was sorry that I asked the question. If we hadn't been in the middle of our pedicures, I would have found a way to gracefully dismiss myself and move on to the next service.

"First, let me say that I have *never* seen Declan with a girlfriend. Not the way he is with you. He's dated a lot. If you haven't noticed, women throw themselves at him. He gets offers all the time."

Irritation clawed through any chance I had of relaxing. I glared at her. "If this conversation has an *upside*, now would be a good time to bring it."

Katherine and Paige also wore disapproving looks.

"I'm not trying to upset you. I was just stating the obvious. You don't see that side; how crazy women can be. I do. I see guys hop in and out of bed like they're rabbits. Declan isn't like that. When he's with you, he's a different person. He isn't caught up in the whole supermodel thing. With you, he's just *Declan*. When he's with you, he's content. *You've* given him that. No other woman has ever done that. He's given his heart to you because you showed him that, after all the superficial crap, he still has one."

My eyes misted at the idea of Declan's contentment because I felt the same.

Aimee paused for a moment and took a sip of her drink. "For you to appreciate the way Declan is, maybe you need to know a little bit about Marisol."

I frowned. Marisol had made herself my enemy. The last thing I wanted to know was more about her, but I let Aimee finish.

"It can be a powerful feeling when people are constantly telling you how beautiful you are. It can really go to your head. Inflate your ego. Declan and I are lucky in that we both had someone to kick us in the backside if we got too full of ourselves. You can find good people in this business and surround yourself with them. That's how we became friends. When we weren't in front of the cameras, we were honest and truthful with one another. We are part of a very small, but tight, group."

"Marisol isn't one of us. She's an egotistical maniac. A creation. She must have been a very lonely little girl. The story goes that she was the fourth of seven children and wasn't very special in her family. She was tall and skinny and picked on in school. I guess, when she was discovered, she was a nice girl. But it went to her head. She believed her own hype. She and her publicist created her persona and Marisol began to believe that she *was* the person she created. In her mind, there is no one above her. She has a completely misguided sense of entitlement. Her balloon took off and no one has been able to pull it back to the ground."

I had a tiny speck of pity for Marisol, but it was more for the child that she was, not the woman she had become.

"How does Declan fit into this? I've seen her with him. She acts like she's dating him, or that she did date him. He says he didn't."

"Ah, now you know how the monster was created, but you don't understand how the monster lives. Marisol believes that whatever she wants, is hers. It's that simple. No one denies her anything. That is, no one except Declan. She doesn't accept rejection; so, in her mind, he hasn't."

"So you're telling me that even though Marisol knows that we're together and in a committed relationship, it means nothing? Does the woman have boundaries?"

"That's *exactly* what I'm saying. Marisol doesn't acknowledge your relationship because, in her mind, there is no relationship. Declan's something she wants and once she gets him, she'll lose interest. You're insignificant. You're just an obstacle."

I had a sick feeling in my stomach. This spa day wasn't turning out the way that it had been intended and I wasn't relaxed at all.

Aimee looked at me. Her face softened. "Now, for the other side of this story ..." She paused for a moment. "I've known Declan my entire modeling career. He's a bit older than me and I've always felt like he's my big brother. I'm telling you the truth. He's changed since he met you. I've never known him to stay away from New York longer than a few days and now he stays away for weeks—*with you.*"

Her words comforted me and blanketed any lingering insecurity. Katherine spoke next.

"Aimee's telling the truth, Aria. He's had me decline invitations. I haven't been working for him for very long. I didn't realize it wasn't the norm."

Paige looked back at me, smiling. Just then, one of the spa staff walked into the room carrying an arrangement of luscious, cream colored roses in a round glass bowl.

"Who's Aria Cole?"

I raised my hand. "I am."

"For you, ma'am."

I looked at Katherine and raised my brow. She put her hands up in the air, refuting any knowledge.

"I didn't have anything to do with this. If they're from Declan, this was all him."

The girls watched me as I opened the envelope and removed the card.

I'm an ass. I don't deserve you.
I love you.
I'm sorry.
Declan

"Well? Are you going to read it to us?" Aimee asked.

I just smiled. "No." I slipped the card in the pocket of my fluffy white robe and shrugged my shoulders. "I just don't know what to make of all of this."

"Oh, I do." A grin spread on Aimee's face from cheek to cheek. "I know exactly what to make of all of this."

CHAPTER
Thirty-Five

Declan

"Yes, Mr. Harris? My plane just landed. Did you get everything you need? Great. Seven o'clock? That's good. I appreciate your assistance."

I retrieved my luggage and had arranged for transport from the airport. I held the cell to my ear. Aria answered on the second ring.

"Hi, beautiful."

"Hi."

"I've missed you."

"I've missed you, too."

The tone was strained. I didn't think either of us wanted to recall our disagreement. The residual tension crackled through the air-waves, making her voice hesitant.

"Still want to go to dinner?"

"I do. Do you?"

"I guess. I'm getting ready now."

"Where are you?"

"At the house. Your house."

I breathed a sigh of relief. The fact that she was at my house meant she wasn't too upset.

"That's good to hear. I'll be there soon.

"Okay." She paused. "Dec?"

"Yeah?"

"I was really pissed, but I did miss you."

Her voice ripped my heart out. Hopefully, Mr. Harris and I had the perfect recipe for damage control.

"Me too, baby. Me too."

CHAPTER
Thirty-Six

Aria

I heard his deep baritone and it cut through any lingering negativity. I was looking forward to the evening. He called out a second time.

"Babe?"

"Up here." I was in the closet finishing with my accessories. By the sound coming from the stairs, it appeared that he was taking them two at a time. Before I stepped out to greet him, his signature scent caressed my senses.

"You didn't hear me downstairs?"

"I was busy getting ready. I'll be out in a minute."

With a final deep breath, I slipped my bright red toes into a pair of pumps and backed out of the closet. As my eyes focused, my body reacted to his presence. I nearly sighed audibly, but managed to halt the sound at my throat. He was dressed in a Tom Ford suit and looked as if he'd just stepped out of one of his ads. The color of the material played up his dark eyes, which were locked on me. He seduced and heated me as his gaze roamed from top to bottom.

"You look beautiful." A grin played at his lips as he lifted my hand to his mouth. He kissed the tops of my fingers and I felt the most delicious warmth flow throughout my whole body, making me blush. I had to throw some cold water on this reunion or we'd never make it to dinner.

"You'll pass."

My response was cheeky. His eyes initially widened in surprise, then narrowed when he guessed what I was doing. There was a hint of warning in his tone.

"Oh, so you're going to be a *bad* girl."

I playfully wrinkled my nose and blinked. "I thought you liked it when I was bad?"

He took a step back, looking amused. "Keep that up and we won't make it out the door."

I returned his look with a devilish one. "Sorry about that. I'll wait until after you've fed me."

A laugh burst from his chest. "I'm going to hold you to that."

He leaned against the wall as I carefully descended the steps. Heels were a rarity for me. I was more comfortable in flats or a pair of Chuck Taylor's, but after the spa I was feeling my girly side.

I bent down for the small black clutch I'd placed on the table. When I went upright, I crashed right into his chest. The connection fired embers that had been suffocated by both disagreement and distance.

He grabbed my shoulders to steady my balance. As his eyes locked with mine, the gold flecks blazed. My skin responded to his touch with a barely detectable shiver.

His tone was deep and smoky. "You okay?"

Words escaped me so I nodded my response.

He led me to the door. When he turned, he blocked my view.

"I know you're not one for jewels, so I got you something I thought you'd like. To say I'm sorry."

He held my hand as we stepped outside. As I looked past him, my eyes caught a hint of red. I froze.

"Oh my god!"

I felt like someone had knocked all of the air from my lungs. I barely had enough oxygen for a whisper. "What have you done?"

Inching my eyes away from the street and onto his face, I saw his expression. A mischievous, evil grin matched the look in his eyes.

"You bought me a building. I bought you a car."

We drove to dinner in a brand-new Mustang. *My* brand-new Mustang. I was speechless for most of the trip. And I surely couldn't drive! I tried to think of all the things I should say, but I couldn't form an argument. I would look out the window and form a thought, then look back at him. When I would open my mouth to say something, he'd look back at me and my words would disappear. I didn't manage to speak a word until we were seated at our table. He just smiled the whole time. It was obvious that he enjoyed my shock.

"I guess I should say thank you?"

It was most definitely a question and not a statement because I really wasn't sure what someone should say when accepting a gift of this magnitude.

"Thank you is a good start."

How can he morph between smug pleasure and suggestive sexuality in a heartbeat? I swallowed. Hard. His eyes never left mine. Over the months that he and I had grown as a couple, I had come to the decision that he was quite the enigma. I solved more of his personal mysteries every day, but even after a year, I was still on a learning curve. A year. *A year? Oh shit! Today is a year!* With everything that had transpired between us, I'd completely forgotten.

"This wrist is a little bare, baby." Declan reached into his pocket and removed a small, soft bag.

"What is this?"

He placed the bag on the table. "Just a little something. Nothing big. Open it."

I picked up the bag and loosened the drawstring. Inside was a

Pandora bracelet with a charm. A silver seashell with a gold starfish.

He took the bracelet from my hand and placed it around my wrist. "It's beautiful, just like you."

"A car *and* a bracelet?"

He leaned back. "The *car* ... we can talk about later."

I raised an eyebrow and smiled. "I'd rather hear about it now, if you don't mind. The 'I bought you a building' statement? That was a business move. Purely strategic. Nothing more, nothing less."

"Then put a logo on the side of the Mustang. You know, for business. Strictly business." A mischievous sarcasm dripped from his tone. "It's already going to get attention. You might as well use it to your advantage." With a very matter-of-fact air, he winked at me.

"That's not why you bought it."

"No. It isn't." He leaned closer and took my hand. "But after the past few days, I think we should learn to trust each other a little more."

I nodded. "I agree, and I do trust you, but ..." I watched as he began to tense. The muscle in his jaw ticked and I didn't want to ruin the evening, so I politely continued. "But ... when it comes to business, it might take a little more time." Not wanting to linger on a sensitive topic, I changed the subject and looked down at my wrist.

"This is a really pretty charm. I know there are lots of them. Why this one?"

"That's easy." He shrugged. "I'm the seashell. You're the starfish."

I laughed. He didn't. His gaze softened and his expression was tender.

"Did you know that the fragile appearance of the starfish is an illusion?" He turned over my hand, causing the charm to rest against my wrist. He placed his finger on it. The move warmed the metal against my skin. "Starfish are completely self-sufficient, but choose to live in pairs. They're survivors. They weather storms because they start out strong. Seashells, on the other hand, look nice but they have rough edges. They need storms to smooth out their edges." He rubbed his thumb against my wrist and looked deep into my eyes. "I picked the charm because it's us. You smooth my rough edges and you ride the waves with me. Strong and beautiful. Like a starfish. I'd like to think that this argument was the first of many storms."

Tears burned my eyes. As he held my hand, the warmth of his smile radiated through me.

"Aria, you're the love I didn't know I was looking for. Your strength is what I need."

"You're not rough." I blinked away the tears as emotion threatened me. "That would be me. You know I was an emotional wreck when we met. My dad's death left me shattered and broken." The irony of his statement made me laugh and sniffle through unshed tears. "And as far as beautiful, *you're* the beautiful one."

"Maybe in a magazine, but you see the real me."

Despite my best effort to maintain my composure, a tear landed on my hand. His sincerity stripped me bare, leaving me vulnerable. "I hate to admit this, but there are times when I feel that I'm not beautiful enough to be with you." The words nearly choked me because they were true.

"Then you have it all wrong. Although I think you're more beautiful than you do, real beauty isn't on the outside. That's just smoke, mirrors, and good marketing. Inside, everyone has an ugliness that isn't so attractive. The only person who really knows me is you. And you love me anyway." He smiled and straightened his shoulders. "Can I tell you something really personal? And don't laugh! Nobody knows this but Carter and me."

I nodded and wiped the dampness from my cheek.

"When I was a little boy, after our dad left, my mom used to tell Carter and me that, when she prayed for us, she was also praying for our future wives. Being little boys, we thought it was gross, but she told us that she believed God already had someone picked out for us. A girl who was as beautiful on the inside as she was on the outside. She asked us to add that little girl to our prayers and to ask God to bless her and watch over her." His eyes misted over. "When my mom passed, she'd pretty much decided that Lacey was that girl for Carter. She was near death when she told Lacey to take care of him; that she'd been praying for her for a long time. When she talked to me about the same subject, she told me that when she went to heaven she would find a way to send the right girl for me." His voice choked with strained emotion. "I believe that's you, Aria."

I took a deep breath and looked up to the ceiling. I'd never felt so emotional and I was afraid I was going to lose my composure and embarrass us both. He gave my hand a light squeeze.

"*You* are my definition of beauty. Everything about you is perfect for me. When I look into your eyes, something magical happens. I become a better man. I *want* to be a better man. *You're* the starfish. If you'll hold on to this rough and ragged seashell, we'll get through the storms. Just like we did with this one. We just have to do it together."

His honesty unhinged me. He was so sincere and hopeful. His words choked me. I could barely raise my voice above a whisper. All I wanted was to get out of the restaurant and be alone with him. I let go of his hand and looked into his eyes, the plea unmistakable.

"Let's go home."

CHAPTER
Thirty-Seven

Declan

S he removed her shoes the moment we arrived at the house. We walked hand-in-hand to the beach side and I let go as she sank her toes into the sand, taking dainty steps.

"I love how cool it feels on my feet." She smiled and performed a few twirls before returning to my side and again entwining our fingers. When we stepped onto the porch, she leaned onto the railing into the salty air. She admired the full moon shining over the water with her chin tipped up.

"It's so beautiful."

Her voice was as gentle as the starlit sky. It was a perfect night, almost as perfect as that first morning in September. The recollection made me realize how much a year had changed us, all for the better. I pressed my chest against her back. My hands roamed from her hips around to her stomach. Her head fell to the side as my lips claimed the sensitive area on her neck where it curved into her shoulder.

"I couldn't agree more." I wasn't referring to the moon, but to the woman before me. My voice betrayed my rising lust. I gathered her hair in my hand and twisted it into my fist. I'd been battling self-control all evening. After the distance that our recent argument had placed between us, being so raw and honest with her in a public place had tested me. Now, with her warmth and my hands on her body, I needed Aria more than I needed air.

She placed her hands over mine and rather than trying to hold them at bay, she pulled them tighter. Her hips pushed back against mine, leaving me no doubt of her desire. *God, I'd missed her!*

As I brought my hand up to her breast, she quietly moaned. That sound was the only encouragement I needed to travel and tease her sexy curves. *This* was contentment and the feeling flooded me. I'd come to realize that I didn't need anything else—just Aria, sea, sky, and sand. Complete euphoria. The two of us in the perfect setting. Mood lighting provided by the full moon, as our bodies moved to the music of crashing waves. Aria's breathing fell in time with my touch. *Perfect.*

I tugged the zipper at the back of her dress lower and lower and kissed from her neck down to the sway of her curves. She shivered as my fingers skated up her skin and slid the dress off of her shoulders. I savored the feel and touch of her skin on my lips as I traveled the same path that was blazed by my fingers. The dress gathered at her hips. I lowered myself into the chair behind me and coasted my hands around her hips and toward her stomach as I pushed it down. It fell at her ankles. I sat back to enjoy the view.

She looked like a goddess in the moonlight. Her dark hair was loose and fell down her breasts and back. The catalogue of emotions from the past few days blended together and ignited my desire.

She started to turn.

"No." She stopped. "I want to look at you."

The strain in my voice betrayed my fragile self control, but the effort I expended toward patience would make the end result so sweet. A painful throbbing pulsed in time with my heart. Subliminal thoughts urged me to take her as my blood and heart beat to their own metronome.

Aria ... beautiful.

Aria ... sexy.

Aria ... mine.

My lips scorched her skin as I leaned forward and kissed her hip. Like the flick of a branding iron, my heat hungered for her tender flesh. I needed her. I ached for her. I wanted to mark her, own her. The more I tasted, the more I wanted. I was under her spell. The lust that she incited infected my blood. Every cell called out her name. I loved the scent of her hair, the touch of her skin, the fullness of her breasts. The delay of our satisfaction caused both pain and pleasure. I was desperate for her and no longer needed to breathe. She was the only life force I needed. I was high with anticipation. She was my universe.

I stood and she turned. I wanted to worship her with the devotion of raw sex. I grabbed her thighs and wrapped her legs around me. We didn't walk; we levitated in a transcendental eroticism. I titillated, seduced, and convinced her that there was no other existence beyond the arousal of our bodies. I licked her heat. Desperation drove me as powerful thrusts submersed me deep inside of her. We became animals. Our urges liquidated conscious thought as we dragged each other toward pleasure. Aria cried out, commanding my body to take her over the edge. Her sweet surrender fed the beast in me and a sound ripped from my chest as she took me with her.

Aria lay in my arms. A transformation had taken place. Something that I felt, but couldn't comprehend. My chest hurt. I loved her to a degree that I didn't think I'd ever understand. *Did I even exist before I knew her? How?*

Her eyes fluttered open. "Hi, Bear."

I pulled her a little closer as her head fit under my chin.

"I want to take you away for a few days." I ran my hand down her arm.

"A vacation? Where?"

"No, not a vacation. A long weekend. I want you to meet Carter and Lacey. A weekend at the lake."

"And the building?" she quizzed.

"We can go there tomorrow. I rode by it today. You were right; it's the perfect location."

My admission made her rise up on her elbow and look at me. An *I told you so* expression was all over her face.

"That look's gonna get you in trouble," I teased.

"That confession's gonna get you in trouble." Laughing, she kissed me lightly on the lips. "I think my new favorite look on you is the one where you tell me that I was right about something."

I sprang into action.

"Declan, stop!" My fingers played at her ribs as I tickled her. "Stop!"

"Only if you promise to be professional about this," I warned.

"I … wasn't … the one … who wasn't … playing … fair." She could barely catch her breath. "STOP!"

I did as she asked and pulled her across my lap until she sat cradled in my arms.

"Aria Cole, I promise to act like a grown-up if you will." I raised three fingers in the air to issue the Boy Scout's promise.

"Does that mean you're going to act like a Boy Scout?" Her grin was devious.

"Whoa! Who said anything about behaving? With you, I'd rather misbehave."

CHAPTER
Thirty-Eight

Aria

Paige and I patiently waited while Declan roamed the building that I'd purchased for him. As he made his inspection, his demeanor remained professional. The wild lover of last night was gone, replaced by a new persona: the *business* Declan. I straightened my posture as he rounded a metal beam.

"Can I take a look at your concept drawing?"

I unrolled the many papers I had filled with rough sketches. As he intensely reviewed my depictions, anticipation rumbled in my stomach. "So, are you proposing that one side of the building be used for a two-level studio or a one-level studio that's divided?"

He sounded so business like. This was a side of him that I wasn't familiar with. He was intense. I could respect that.

"I'm suggesting a one-level studio, divided into two parts, with a large partition. You can pull the partition open for a large photo session. Pull it closed and you have two smaller studios." I pointed to the imaginary wall. "One large window would be shared by both spaces. If the window covering is motorized, you could control the amount of natural light with a remote control." I supported the suggestion by pulling the vendor information and handed him the pamphlets on partitions and motorized window coverings. He paused for a moment and looked them over.

"On this drawing, you've added a second floor. The room dimensions are marked, but I'd like to hear some more detail."

"Yes, certainly." My nerves were exposed in the tone of my reply. My arm crossed over his as I pointed to one side of the drawing. "Right here? The second floor would be used for offices and other needed space. The front of the building, the side where the view of the bay can best be seen? That's where your office and a conference room would be. If you put the workspaces in cubicles around the interior walls, you'd have double the workspace for make-up and hair areas. Outside walls would house smaller offices with windows. You could use those however you like. It maximizes the space. And down here?" I pointed to the lower level sketch. "This space could be dual-purposed as a lunchroom or a small entertainment space, like a cock-tail party."

He examined my layout with a stern eye. As a nervous response, I grew chatty.

"Look. You can see here the space I've designated toward the highway. That can be the lobby. See here? I've marked these dimensions to accommodate a reception desk and a large marquee wall. For your business name. And here? Ample seating for visitors and clients. Here? The double doors access the entrance from your parking lot, which would be directly from the highway side."

I was pointing everywhere as his eyes darted across the pages. I tried to hide my trembling. I had never felt such angst with a client and consoled myself with the reminder that if he didn't share the vision, I had alternate plans for the building. I really wanted him to like it, but I struggled to maintain a professional demeanor. Paige had been our silent spectator and I was sure she could sense my stress. When we locked eyes, she attempted to diffuse the situation.

"Well, Declan. What do you think of Aria's plan?" He paused at her question, then turned toward me. At first his expression was stern, his gaze hard. Then he placed his hand over mine. His eyes softened and he broke into a satisfied, yet ruthless grin. *Like a shark!*

"I think my woman is a visionary genius." He paused and pulled me hard against his chest. "And I'm the luckiest man in the world to have her as my partner."

I melted. *So much for business!*

"Do you really like it?" I breathed a huge sigh of relief.

"Like it? That would be an understatement." The praise fell freely from his lips. "It's beyond anything I'd envisioned. Your parents were right; you do have an artist's eye." He bent to kiss me. "I'm sorry I underestimated you. You're very talented." He kissed me. "Forgive me?" His sexy baritone poured over me.

"Does this mean I get the job?"

"Not only do you get the job …" His tone grew serious. "I want you to be my partner. You can choose to be a silent one if you want, but I want your name on the paperwork of the business."

I was flabbergasted. "I'm flattered. Truly, I am. But I want you to have your own business. I'm content to be part of the renovation."

"No. I'll think of a compelling argument, but I want you as a partner. I wouldn't be doing this if you hadn't been the one to push it."

"I'm not looking for another business. I like the one I have." I placed my hands on his lapels and looked up into his eyes. "I do, however, have a few ideas on how you can apologize for doubting my abilities." Roaming hands joined my suggestive comment.

Paige cleared her throat as a reminder that she was still in the room.

CHAPTER
Thirty-Nine

Aria

"I can't tell you how good it is to finally meet the woman who's taming my brother." Carter gave me a big hug.

"Get your big paws off her!" Declan raised his voice, but he was joking. He pushed his brother away and wrapped his arms around me. Carter's dog was running around in circles, barking in response to the raised voices. I bent over to pet her.

"Who are you, precious?" I sank my hands into a generous amount of fur.

"That's our Cody-girl." A woman with blonde hair, that I recognized from FaceTime visits, approached me with a bright smile. *Lacey.* "She's the biggest bundle of hair and love you'll ever see." She placed her hands on my shoulders and pulled me into a soft embrace. Her touch was so light; it was the gentlest hug I could remember. Then she held me out at arm's length and looked me over. "Aria, I'm so happy you're here. It feels like I've known you forever with those phone chats, but nothing beats getting up close and personal."

"I agree. I'm so happy to meet you."

"Hey, what about me?" Declan gestured with his thumbs pointed toward his chest. I moved out of the way.

"I could never forget my favorite brother-in-law." Her voice was unmistakably exuberant as she gave him a big hug. He laughed and kissed her on the cheek.

"I'm your *only* brother-in-law, Lace. Of course I'm your favorite."

"Caught me." There was a twinkle in her eye as she winked at him. Then she pointed to our luggage.

"Don't worry about your bags. Carter will take them up to your room." She placed herself between us and threaded her arms through ours. "Are you hungry? You had a long drive."

As she walked us toward the dining room the most delicious mix of smells seduced us.

"I made pot roast, mashed potatoes, asparagus, salad, and some homemade rolls. Carter has some red and white wines, if you like." She then leaned toward Declan. "And I'm guessing your brother knows what you want to drink."

"Lace, you're killing me!" He mocked distress. "You're going to get me fired."

Lacey pushed his arm and he fell back, faking injury.

I shot him a warning look to remind him to be polite. "We'd love dinner. Pay no attention to the fool beside me." I shook my head as Declan held a chair out for me. I took in a deep lungful of the savory scents. "Everything smells delicious."

My comment put a huge smile on Lacey's face. The sound of heavy footsteps grew louder as Carter descended the stairs and joined us in the dining room.

"Please tell me that both of you are hungry. If not, she'll make me eat leftovers for a week," he pleaded.

"Stop being so dramatic, hotshot, and grab the drinks." Lacey playfully narrowed her eyes at her handsome husband.

"Yes, my love." His tone was patronizing. When she turned her back to him he looked at both of us and shrugged his shoulders. His voice lowered. "I gotta do what she says. Have you heard that bullshit about *happy wife, happy life?"*

———————◆———————

The meal was incredible. I was so full that I felt uncomfortable and unbuttoned the top of my jeans. Lacey led me into the family room. Carter and Declan offered to clean up and shooed us away by telling us to go have a little girl time.

"That was an incredible meal. Thank you."

She waved me off. "It's nothing. I love to cook. I don't get to do much in the winter with school in session and September is the unofficial start of winter up here in the mountains. I appreciate being able to cook for more than just the two of us. When I'm working, I cook mostly crockpot meals." She moved toward the sofa. "C'mon over here. Kick off your shoes and get comfy. You're family." She patted the cushion and the dog jumped up.

"Hey! You're not supposed to be up here!"

The dog completely ignored the scold and positioned herself between us.

"I don't mind, really." I loved the feel of her soft fur. My hand disappeared into her neck as I petted her. "She's so fluffy. She looks like a friendly bear."

"She's a Bernese Mountain Dog. They do look like bears. We have to be careful where she runs during hunting season. She doesn't have a mean bone in her body; she's the friendliest cuddle bug you could ever love." She looked from the dog to me. "Are you sure you're okay with her being up here with us? Some people don't like dogs getting so close."

"Absolutely!" I had already fallen in love with the dog. She was like a gigantic stuffed animal right next to me.

Lacey watched me. "You remind me a lot of my mother-in-law. She was very tender-hearted like you." A hint of reflection graced her tone. I leaned back against the pillows and tucked my toes beneath Cody's warm coat.

"Declan doesn't talk much about his mom. Only once, really."

"Rose was one of the most wonderful people in the world. I wish there were more people like her. Especially more mothers. Being a teacher, I see too much sometimes. Her boys were her world. She adored them. She went through a lot when their dad left."

"What would make you think I'm like her?"

"I can see it in your eyes. When Rose loved, she did it with her whole heart. There's no doubt that you're all in. I can see that you're in love with him."

"Am I that transparent?"

"Maybe not to the boys, but you are to me." She took a sip of her tea and adjusted a blanket across her lap. "You know, Rose and I became really close when I married Carter. The more I got to know her, the more I respected her strength. Our friendship went well beyond birthdays, Christmas, and exchanging recipes—though she was a great cook. Our friendship shaped me. When I met Carter, I was such a people pleaser. She taught me that, no matter what you do, you can't please everyone. She was such a good mentor. When she knew that she didn't have much longer, she told me that I picked up where she left off in loving her son. She told me not to be afraid to love him fearlessly—that love is always worth it. That's what I am telling you. Don't be afraid to love Declan with your whole heart. The costs of loving him, no matter what they are now, or in the future, will be worth it. The Sinclairs are good men."

I got up from the sofa to hug her. She put her hand on the back of my head like I was a child, her voice full of emotion in a broken whisper.

"Rose would have loved you."

We separated at the sound of footsteps. Declan and Carter walked into the room. Their laughs preceded them, but when they saw Lacey and me, they grew serious. Carter's look of concern bounced between us.

"Is everything okay?"

We looked at each other knowingly and both dabbed at our eyes. Lacey smiled at him.

"Everything's perfect."

CHAPTER
Forty

Declan

"Okay. That's a wrap. Good job, everyone."

The photo session had come to an end. As I approached, Jonatan was removing the camera strap from his neck. I lightly slapped his back. "Thanks for making the session go so smoothly, man."

"That was all you, Dec. I thought all hell was going to break loose when Marisol started in with the smart-ass comments, but you held it together. She was such a bitch the way she was baiting you. If it had been me, I don't know that I could've kept my mouth shut."

I nodded. "But we're used to her, right? And we got the job done."

From the corner of my eye, I saw Aimee approach. She was one of five models on this shoot. She gave us both a peck on the cheek.

"I'm going to go change, guys. Thanks for a good session."

We watched as she walked away. Jon nodded toward her as he stuffed a cord in a bag. "She's a real sweetheart."

"Yeah, she is. She's a pain in my ass sometimes, because she's like my little sister."

After the set was broken down and all the models had changed, I ducked into a room for privacy so that I could phone Aria.

"Hey, babe. Aimee and I just finished up. How's everything coming with the studio?"

"Couldn't be better. We're actually running ahead of schedule. I'm so excited for you to see the changes. It's been a long couple of months, but I think we'll be finished in two weeks or so."

"That is good news! I'm going to get together with Aimee and plan some time to put the word out. She has a few friends in marketing. She said they were eager to work with me. I need to talk to them about advertising and then I'm coming home. I've missed you, baby."

"Miss you too, Bear."

She said her nickname for me in a quiet voice. She was at a construction site. I strained to hear her because of the noise in the background.

"I'll see you soon."

I disconnected our call and punched in Aimee's number. I was hoping to catch her for a cup of coffee before we met with the advertisers. With my cell on speaker, I reached over to snatch up my bag. I felt someone tap me on the shoulder and turned.

Marisol!

"Leaving so soon?"

She wore a sinister smile, which immediately brought out my worst side. "I have plans."

As I tried to walk around her, she blocked me. "Want to have dinner with me?"

"No, thanks. Like I said, I have plans."

I tried to go in the opposite direction and she blocked me again.

"What have I done to offend you? You never pay attention to me anymore. I never see you outside of work and you never stay around to talk to me after sessions. I'm starting to think you don't like me."

"I'm starting to think you don't get it," I curtly replied. "I told you before, we just work together."

She stuck out her bottom lip in a pout. "We were friends."

"We were never more than friends, if that."

"Friends with benefits."

"That's bullshit! I never touched you!"

"You wanted to!"

"You're a crazy bitch! I never said that."

"You never had to. I saw the way you looked at me. You know you wanted me."

"You really are delusional. If I ever gave you that impression, it was because I was drunk or high. Nothing else."

"I could have made it more!" She grabbed onto my sleeve as I tried to walk away. I jerked my arm away from her hold.

"Only in your own twisted mind. Get it straight! I'm involved with someone. A beautiful woman."

"Twisted?" She cackled like a witch. "*You're* the one who's twisted. You don't know what beautiful is. I've seen your little sea bitch!"

"You're sick and malicious—and you're taking my time."

I walked away and felt something whiz by my ear. I turned to see her glare. *Crazy bitch!* I left her standing there and kept on walking. When I got outside, I found Aimee. A concerned look was on her face.

"What took you so long?"

"Marisol. She had a meltdown."

"What did you do?" Her expression graduated from concern to worry.

"Blew her off."

"I'm not sure that was wise."

"What the hell would you want me to do? She's certifiable."

"Yeah; but she scares me, Dec. I'm not sure her crossing the lines is all an act. Like, she might really have problems."

"I'm not worried about her."

"Maybe you should be. She obsesses about you. If you're not worried about yourself, maybe you should think about Aria."

"You worry too much. Let's get some coffee and talk business," I said, changing the subject.

"Okay, but don't say I didn't warn you."

Aimee had it all under control and her friends had a great plan. After she filled me in at the coffee shop, we met at their office. The marketing was brilliant and I couldn't wait to share everything with Aria.

"Hey, babe, I'm on my way now. My meeting is finished. Do you think three weeks is enough time to pull this whole thing together?"

"Three weeks is good. I'm done. The guys are just finishing up. Do you have the decorator's number? I can call them."

"Yeah, I'll send you the contact information. Now that we're finished, let's take a break."

"Everything looks good on this end. What do you have in mind?"

"Are you sure we're ready?" I was a worrier and this business was my first big deal. Aria had kept us ahead of schedule, so we would be up and running in weeks rather than months.

"Yes! Stop worrying."

"I'm not worrying. I just can't see what's going on from here. I want to be on top of things."

"You're a control freak. Everything's fine."

"Good. Now, go throw some stuff in a bag and meet me at Carter and Lacey's."

"Really?"

Apparently the prospect of seeing my brother and his wife was an idea she liked. "They're expecting us. I'll meet you there. Aimee and I aren't far from there. She said she'll drop me off before she heads to New York."

"I'm heading home now. Maybe when you get there, you can chill out."

There was definitely sarcasm in that comment. "Call me before you leave, baby. It's a long drive and you're not used to driving the mountain roads."

"I will. Promise."

CHAPTER
Forty-One

Marisol

*W*hat the hell is his problem?

Marisol watched as Declan and Aimee left the coffee shop. Her investigator had given her the inside information on Declan and Aria's business, but she didn't understand what he was trying to accomplish. Why would he want to open a business in Maryland when he had New York? He had everything. Money, clothes, prestige … *me*. What more could he want?

Declan didn't like working with her anymore; he preferred working with Aimee. The more he excluded her, the more she wanted to be included. It was becoming apparent that he didn't need her the way he used to and she didn't like that. At all. In fact, she didn't like the idea of him doing *anything* without her. He had become evasive. When she asked direct questions, he never gave direct answers. It was hard to keep tabs on him without the assistance of a professional. The more she didn't know about Declan's activities, the more she wanted to know. But Mr. Richards's information wasn't coming fast enough. That was why she tagged Declan's bag with a transmitter.

It was a brilliant idea, really. Mr. Richards was useful in that regard. He had connections that enabled her to get the equipment she wanted. Nothing noticeable, just something little that allowed her to overhear conversations. Once Declan went into the shop with Aimee, all she had to do was stay a reasonable distance away and she could hear their entire conversation. It was the best money she had ever spent and was the best way to keep tabs on Declan. He hadn't gotten that girl out of his system. It was imperative that she know why.

It bothered her that Declan was still with Aria. She couldn't understand what he saw in her. They had nothing in common. *So what was it?* The thought of Declan in bed with that girl made her sick to her stomach. *All that flesh!* She would never understand why men liked girls with all that fat on them.

The most recent report from Mr. Richards had been delivered before the shoot. It wasn't until she watched Declan walk away that she'd had time to read it. Now that she had, she wasn't happy. It was only logical to follow Declan and Aimee. She had chosen a seat near the door. Neither of them noticed her when she came in. She left just as inconspicuously. Vicious anger joined her on the walk to get a car.

So Declan and Aimee are going to set up a satellite company. What a joke! He can't pick a beautiful woman for himself. Who wants to see what he picks for the industry?

It was time to form a plan to destroy Declan's dream. Then he would come back to the life he had before the bitch. Aimee didn't concern her. She was just a tiny piss ant in the world of beauty. There were women like her everywhere. She was a *filler;* she filled seats at award shows and was called in to model whenever someone better couldn't make it. *Of course she would offer to assist Declan! Between the two of them they had one brain!*

The part of the conversation that Marisol found most interesting was when Aimee said that Declan should take her seriously. She detected fear in Aimee's voice. *She should be afraid!* Marisol had the connections to have Aimee blackballed. She would use them if necessary, but she would rather use her. *If she and Aria were friends, maybe Aimee would warn her.*

As she brought the espresso to her mouth, the paper cup was kissed by her lipstick. It wouldn't be that hard to get Declan under control; he wasn't very smart. She would have him, his beach house, and his business. All she had to do was exercise patience. The first step was to follow him. He never went anywhere without his bag and now that the transmitter was connected to it, she was privy to all of his plans. She could hear enough to ruin his life and cause chaos.

A rush of power flooded her with pleasure. It would take very little effort to incorporate misery into his private and business lives. And when it was all over, *when the bitch was gone,* he would thank her for it.

CHAPTER
Forty-Two

Aria

"*Lacey's dead ...*"

I kept hearing the words in a never-ending loop in my head. I was only fifty miles away from the lake house when I called Carter's cell to see if Declan and Aimee had arrived. He answered the phone with a fury that I didn't recognize.

"*What?*"

"*Carter? What's wrong?*"

"*It's ... Lacey's dead.*"

I couldn't remember what I said after that. He kept talking. I remember hearing his voice through his tears, but I couldn't retain many of the details. My mind struggled to recall his words as I kept driving. I went straight through a red light. I remember telling him that I'd be there as soon as I could, but after that, everything was a blur. I didn't know if Declan was there, but at least we were both on our way to Carter. That was the goal. Get to Carter.

When I heard the voice of my GPS, I realized that I was almost at my destination. I had driven for almost fifty miles without realizing it. Shock must have had that effect on me. I kept hearing Carter's words over and over in my head. I knew that I would learn the details as soon as I got there, but I was hoping this was a terrible mistake.

My tires crunched in the stone driveway. I saw Carter's and Lacey's cars, two State Trooper vehicles, and Aimee's car. Declan must have heard me pull in because as soon as I turned off the ignition, he bolted out the front door. I stepped out of the car; my knees turned to jello and he ran toward me.

"Are you okay, baby?" He searched my face. I only managed a nod as my eyes filled with tears.

"Please tell me that this is not happening!"

His eyes filled with tears of his own. His voice was cracked and broken. "I wish I could ..."

His voice trailed off. He looked like he could barely breathe.

"I'm so sorry." I held him close while he buried his face in my hair.

"Aimee and I ... we didn't know anything. We hung around the coffee shop for a while because I knew it would take you a couple of hours. I shouldn't have ... I could have been here." Frustration choked him.

"You didn't know!"

"I was worried about you. I didn't want to be in the mountains if you had to call me. I was worried about the signal ..." He pushed me back and held me at arms length. His eyes looked me over from top to bottom. "Are you okay?"

"I'm fine." I moved closer and wrapped my hands around his waist. "I want to go in and see Carter."

"Yeah." His shoulders sagged. As he draped his arm around my shoulders, we made the solemn walk from the driveway to the house. The black night reeked with a deathly scent and we breathed it in. The hinges creaked as Declan pushed open the door.

All of the joy that I'd experienced here previously was gone. There wasn't a speck of it left within the walls. No air of happiness, not even a slight smile. Even Cody wasn't herself. She knew that something was wrong. She lay curled up in a ball by Carter's feet.

She didn't get up when we entered the room. All she could manage was to raise her eyes. Carter didn't even do that. He just stared blankly at the floor.

I quietly walked over to him and knelt down. Placing my hands on his knees, I looked up into his pained face. He looked like he had aged twenty years since I'd seen him a few months ago.

"Hi."

"Hi." He put his hand on my shoulder and looked at me with red-rimmed eyes. "I'm glad you're here."

"Me too." I squeezed his knee.

A noise came from the kitchen and I turned around. Aimee gave me a weak smile. I looked up at Carter.

"I'll be right back."

When I walked into the kitchen, Aimee held out her arms. "Hey girl." Her voice was a reverent whisper.

"Hey." As we separated, she turned toward the counter.

"Are you hungry? I'll make you a sandwich."

I shook my head. "I don't have an appetite." I looked toward the sofa where Carter was still sitting. "Has he said much?"

"No. He's been like that since we got here. The State Troopers brought him back here after he identified her body. They arrived at the same time we did."

"I didn't know. I called him to see if you were here. He lost it."

"Yeah. I can only imagine."

Aimee walked over and stuffed a Kleenex into my hand. We looked at Carter. Declan had moved next to him and had his hand on his brother's back. My heart was torn. Carter's tear-streaked face was haggard and Declan didn't look much better.

"Thanks for driving him here. I don't know how he's going to handle this. He and Lacey were very close."

"I'm staying in case you all need anything. Go on in with them. I'll be here."

I nodded and moved to the living room, sitting next to Declan. He slipped his arm around my waist. I leaned forward.

"How are you doing, Carter?"

He raised his tired eyes to me and ignored the tears that had begun to freely fall.

"I'm numb. I can't believe it. I don't want to live without her."

Cody heard the anguish in his voice and placed her head in his lap. Absent-mindedly, he placed his hand on her head. Pain poured off of him. "The person that hit her never stopped. They just left her. How could they do that??" He looked down at the floor again and shook his head in disbelief. "She knew everyone was coming. She said she was going to get some fresh air. It was just a bike ride." He looked at me. "Someone driving up the road saw her. They called 911. By the time ..." His voice cracked and he crumbled. As he held his head in his hands, the sobs ripped from his chest.

Declan and I broke down as well. We both loved them. Seeing Carter like this was as devastating as Lacey's loss.

"She was always careful when she rode." He shook his head in disbelief as his voice wavered. "She *never* went out without her helmet. She didn't stand a chance. She was only a hundred and twenty-two pounds." He turned to us and raised his hands. "What possible match is a hundred and twenty-two-pound woman against a car!" The desperate sobs choked him. "How? Tell me, please!*"*

He shot out of his seat and started pacing. Declan walked over to him and threw his arms around his brother. They searched each other's faces. Carter took a deep breath, and with a heart-wrenching plea, he looked to Declan for solace.

"Do you want to know what's killing me? What's tearing me apart? I wonder how long she was lying there in pain ... alive ... hurt ... just praying that someone would come. A minute? An hour? Did she wonder where I was? Did she try to reach her phone? Was she in too much pain?" Carter shook Declan and yelled so loud that everyone jumped. "Did the heartless son of a bitch care that she died alone?" He disintegrated, collapsing into Declan's arms. He couldn't breathe through his cries and held his chest. "I didn't know it would be the last time I'd see her. I didn't kiss her goodbye. I didn't even tell her I loved her."

Declan struggled to hold his brother who was equal in size. Both were emotionally shredded. Aimee rushed in from the kitchen and the four of us held onto each other while we exhausted our sorrow.

We finally managed to get Carter onto the family room sofa. He refused to sleep in their bed. Cody lay down on the floor next to him, standing guard over her master. I removed his shoes while Aimee got a blanket. He needed whatever amount of sleep his poor body would take. Then the three of us moved into the kitchen to talk quietly. Declan's face was full of anguish.

"I feel so helpless. I loved her. She was my sister, but I can only imagine what Carter …" He stopped; clearing his throat, he tried again. "He needs me, but I don't know what to do."

Declan ran his hands through his hair. I placed my hand over his heart. "You're doing the best thing that you can. You're here for him." I moved my hand to his cheek and his pain-filled eyes looked into mine. "And I'm here for you."

His voice was barely audible. "I don't know what I'd do if it were you …"

"Shhhh …" I put my finger to his lips as a vice clenched my heart. "Don't go there. Just be here for him." I tilted my head in the direction of the family room and managed a weak smile. He pulled me in and closed his arms around me. I buried my face in his chest and held him just as tightly. He laid his head on mine. The sound of his velvet baritone had been raked raw with sorrow.

"If I ever find the person who did this, I'll kill them."

CHAPTER
Forty-Three

Aria

The funeral of Lacey Sinclair was a bittersweet occasion. Countless people turned out to give tribute to a woman who was loved, honored, and treasured. From local dignitaries, including the town's Mayor and Chief of Police, to her former students, each person struggled with the loss and gave tearful testimony of the shining example that Lacey's life offered to all.

Declan thought he was prepared for his brother's reaction to laying his wife to rest, but he was unprepared for his own. The struggle was evident. Pain formed circles around his eyes. He battled with and lost his emotions. Tears traveled down the etched lines in his granite expression. Carter managed to keep his emotions in check while in public. His fellow Troopers stood around him in a strong wall of protection. There was a poignant strength in their presence that everyone tapped into at the gravesite.

As the minister said prayers over Lacey's remains, one of her friends sang *a capella*. The lyrics of *In the Garden* drifted from the soloist's lips toward heaven as everyone stood silently, sniffling into tissues.

Once the service was concluded, all were welcomed to honor

Lacey's memory at a luncheon in the town hall. The crowd was larger than anticipated, but Aimee had taken care of everything and assured Carter that he needn't be concerned. She had ordered more than enough food from the caterer and had also coordinated the gifts of prepared food from friends and neighbors. She'd gone ahead to play hostess for the family while Declan stayed behind with Carter.

"Please, take Aria and go on without me. I'd like to stay here with Lacey just a little while longer." His vocal chords had been taxed by his cries the night before. The sound coming out of him barely resembled his strong tone.

Declan shook his head at his brother. "No, we'll wait for you."

Carter shot him a stern look. There was a simmering anger lying just underneath the anguish. "I need a little more time to say goodbye, Dec. Can't you understand that? Dammit, give me some space!"

Aria intervened, inserting herself between the two of them. With emotions riding sky high, she didn't want them relieving their tension by taking it out on each other.

"Calm down. He just didn't want you to be by yourself." Her voice softened as she placed her hands on Carter's arms and pushed him away from his brother. "He loves you. He's just concerned." She exchanged glances with both of them. "Lacey wouldn't want you two to go at each other, especially not today."

They both softened at the invocation of Lacey's name. As the words sank in, they nodded in agreement.

"I'd like a few moments alone with Lacey. I've asked one of my friends from the force to stay behind. He'll drive me to meet up with you. That's him over there." As he pointed toward a Trooper in uniform, the officer tipped his hat. Carter's posture sagged against the wooden chair. The shadow under the canopy made him appear older than his age. "Look, I've been surrounded by people twenty-four seven for the past two days. I haven't had a minute to myself. Everything has been about the funeral arrangements or someone wanting to say something about her." His jaw slackened as he looked at the casket. A spray of roses lay on top. He leaned forward and cupped one of the buds in his hand. "I need to talk to her. *Alone*." He looked up, the torment in his eyes nearly palpable. "Please understand ..."

Aria squeezed Declan's hand, whispering reverently. "He'll be fine."

Resigned, Declan approached his brother, stooping low. He clasped his arm tightly. "Love you, bro. Take all the time you need."

Carter's eyes filled with tears. "Yeah, me too. I'll see you in a little while."

They walked toward the ebony limousine as Carter pulled his chair closer to the coffin. He bowed his head far enough to rest it against the wood. It was apparent that a private conversation was taking place between him and the woman with whom he'd shared his life ... before he would let them put her body into the ground.

The familiar splintering of death invaded Aria's heart. She knew that the days ahead wouldn't be kind. Losing someone was never easy, but the passage of time would make the loss easier to bear.

Marisol watched from the shadows. She wasn't celebrating Lacey's life, she was celebrating how clever she was that no one recognized her or thought to ask for her name. The events had played in her favor and she relished the heavy atmosphere surrounding Declan and his family. She mingled with the crowd, blending in as best she could. When everyone had dispersed, she moved to a safe distance to watch as grief gave her a winning hand in her game.

She went unnoticed behind a large, marble tombstone and moved closer as Carter rose from his chair. She walked past the man in uniform who was obviously waiting for him. It was now or never.

"Carter?"

"Yes."

"I don't want to interrupt you. I'm a friend of your brother's. I heard what happened and attended to pay my respects. I just wanted to tell you how sorry I am for the loss of your wife."

"Thanks. That's very kind of you." His mind was numb, having repeated the same phrase over a hundred times. "Would you like to join us for lunch?"

"No, no." She plastered a pleasant smile on her face to give the illusion that she cared. "That's why I stayed behind. I have to run, but I didn't want to leave without saying goodbye and extending my condolences." She took his hand and patted it for effect.

"Thanks for coming."

"Think nothing of it."

Carter walked with her until his friend approached and diverted his attention. The woman got into the passenger's side of her car and waved. He waved back as she pulled away, the other man looking in her direction.

"Who was that?"

"I don't know. Some friend of Declan's."

CHAPTER
Forty-Four

Declan

After Lacey's funeral, I immersed myself in the preparations for the opening of the new business. Katherine and I had finished for the day and went to meet Aria and Paige at the Stoney Lonen Pub for a late lunch. Aria had just completed the renovation of a small beach cottage nearby and Paige had been showing property in the area. The coincidence of all of us being in the same vicinity was rare, so we took the opportunity to get together. As Katherine and I walked in, the owners, Brian and Rita, waved and pointed to the booth that Aria and Paige occupied. Aria scooted over to make room for me, as Katherine took a seat beside Paige.

"Hi, beautiful." I gave Aria a quick kiss.

"Hi." Delight danced in her blue eyes. "You two look happy."

Katherine gave Aria and Paige a wide smile as I filled them in on what we'd been doing. "We've been going over the details of the opening. The guest list is long, but since Aimee knows most of the people, she said she would take care of the invitations. She suggested that we invite everyone we've worked with over the years and I agree. Her philosophy is that no one's ever offended if they're invited and decline; they're only offended if they're *not* invited."

Aria wrinkled her nose and made a face.

"I suppose that means we have to invite Marisol …" It was both a question and a statement.

"We don't *have* to invite her. This is your night as much as it's mine. I don't care what Marisol thinks if she isn't on the guest list. I do care whether or not you have a good time. If you don't want her there, just say the word." I reached across the table and took her hand in mine.

Aria had worked hard on the project and her ideas were brilliant. The changes in the space were astonishing. It had gone from an empty shell to a gorgeous structure. If we hadn't documented the work with photographs, people would never believe that the building was formerly a gym. I was confident that the business would entice even the most reserved clients because it was perfect. I was proud of Aria. The fact that I was in love with such a visionary was an added bonus. Her gaze met mine.

"I don't want her excluded because of me. It would be obvious that there's bad blood. That's not good for business."

"You're amazing; you know that?" I leaned over and gave her a long kiss. When our lips parted, I became lost in her eyes.

"Hello. We're still here." Katherine playfully interrupted, reminding us that we weren't alone. "Could you please save that stuff for later? We've got a grand opening to plan."

Aria and I smiled at each other before I turned to my assistant and raised my brows. "You were saying …"

"Yes, I was saying that the invitations go out tomorrow. Everything's set—the menu, music, even a red carpet. This is going to be epic! Probably the biggest event this little town's ever seen!"

I turned to Aria. "It's been work, but it's been fun. All that's left to do is to choose your dress."

"What?" Aria looked like a deer in headlights. "I don't know what I'm wearing yet."

"I've chosen three gowns from my favorite designers. I want you to look at them and try them on. Hopefully, you'll like them. I'll choose my tux based on what you wear."

She searched my eyes. "That's too extravagant."

"No, it isn't," I argued. "None of this would have been possible without you. Her eyes changed as she warred with her emotions. Witnessing the tempestuous storm was always an experience. As the hues changed to shades of ocean blue, I knew that she had decided to let me have my way. Her smile widened until the corners of her mouth nearly met the corners of her eyes.

"Okay. You win."

CHAPTER
Forty-Five

Aria

"I'm coming down!"

I called to Declan from upstairs. I felt like Cinderella going to the ball. I looked at myself in the full-length mirror. The woman reflecting back at me was beautiful. My long, dark waves had been styled in a way that part of my hair was up and some hung down. I had a sparkling starfish clip in my hair, made from a pin that had belonged to Declan's grandmother. Aimee had done my make-up several hours before. She had made my eyes smoky, so that the blue was much more intense than usual. My lips were dark red to match my dress.

Michelle Nagem, a new designer whom Declan declared as *the next big thing*, had designed my gown. It was the deepest shade of garnet, with a blue tone. Strapless on one side and looping the other, it accentuated my breasts. The dress fit my torso like a glove and split at the waist into two pieces, making the one side look like a long pleat. It all flowed together to form an elegant puddle at my feet. As I walked, the gown sashayed and showed my matching sandals. I wore simple diamond earrings to complete the ensemble.

Yes, the woman staring back at me was surely Cinderella. I

hoped that I wouldn't turn into a pumpkin.

As I neared the bottom of the stairs, Declan said nothing. For several minutes his eyes rested on me and I didn't know how to gauge his reaction. When his eyes finally met mine, I was surprised to see them misty. My heart raced at his display of emotion.

"How did I ever get so lucky?" He lifted my hand and kissed the back of it, a gesture that never failed to make me feel like a princess. "I have something for you," he said, reaching into his pocket. He pulled out a box. "Open it."

I did as requested. Inside was a dainty bracelet with a diamond-encrusted starfish. "Is this for tonight?"

"I thought it would be appropriate." He fastened it around my wrist.

"It's so pretty and it isn't overdone." I tilted my chin to welcome his kiss. "I love it."

"All eyes will be on you tonight." His eyes narrowed. "I might get violent if the men get too close."

I shook my head and laughed at him. *Did he even hear himself?* The most beautiful people in the fashion industry would be there tonight. I seriously doubted that I'd be a visible threat, especially in a room filled with supermodels. The old saying "love is blind" came to mind.

"You truly don't see how beautiful you are, do you?" He placed his forehead on mine. "That's another reason why I love you. You are the most genuine person I've ever known."

I could feel the honesty in his words, but now wasn't the time to get lost in them. This was his night.

"You're sweet and a little crazy, but stop. We have a party to go to."

"Don't tell me to stop. You have no idea how refreshing it is to see a beautiful woman blush when she's paid a compliment. Most of the people I know are so used to it that it doesn't faze them. You'll get a taste of it tonight, so be prepared." He placed a kiss against my throat. My pulse raced beneath his lips. "I feel like the luckiest man to be taking *you* to the gala. Men will want you; women will want to be you."

I laughed.

"I'm telling the truth," he said, smiling at me. "Yes, Declan; they will, because I'll be with *you*."

"I love you; you know that?"

His eyes held a promise. He was *my* Prince Charming.

"I have one more thing to say and then we'll go: any woman can put on clothes and make-up, but you can't beautify an ugly soul." His eyes were loving as he looked into mine. I was drowning in their sincerity. He lifted my arm and placed it through his as he escorted me to the door. I heard him speak under his breath.

"I really am one lucky son-of-a bitch …"

CHAPTER
Forty-Six

Aria

Hollywood came to the ocean for one night. Declan and I arrived in our stretch limousine and it was as if a whole new world opened up to me. There were spotlights on the gigantic letters that hung on the concrete wall above the doorway. It was beautiful. *The Studio*. Declan said that the name was simple and perfect, as if it were the only studio in existence. To us, it was.

I felt like a movie star draped on the arm of my handsome escort. Photographers were everywhere, and for a brief time, I imagined what it must be like to have the paparazzi constantly following your every move. Reporters, both local and national, called his name. From Entertainment Television to WRDE, their attempts to get his attention were relentless as they competed for a photo or a brief interview. The elite in social media converged on our little town. Although the air was electrified, Declan remained calm and composed. He was in his element. Several times, he leaned in to kiss my cheek or nuzzle my neck allowing for a photo op of the two of us. One thing was for sure, if anyone was unaware that Declan and I were in a relationship, tonight's public displays removed all doubt.

When we entered the building, we were immediately impressed

with the fabulous job that Katherine had done. Her attention to detail had made The Studio an East Coast showpiece. We sought her out to commend her for her hard work. While Declan told her how impressed he was with every detail, I quietly stood at his side. Then it was time to mingle with his guests, but Declan assured me that Katherine would be well-rewarded for her efforts. I loved his thoughtfulness for his assistant while in the midst of the most impressive people in his world.

A man approached and Declan spoke near my ear.

"My agent. Blake Matthews."

He looked more like a model than an agent. As I watched him approach, I saw that he held the hand of Marisol and was leading her toward us as well.

She was stunning. Her ice blue gown showcased her dark Latin looks. There were no signs of distress on her beautiful face, though anxiety played at my nerves. Marisol was cool, calm, and breathtaking.

"This is an impressive gathering, Declan. The buzz I've heard is all good. Some of the clients are already making plans. You should be very proud. You know how discriminating they can be. If you've gotten their approval, it shows you had the right idea."

The praise obviously meant a lot to Declan by the look on his face. He beamed and slid his arm around my waist.

"Thank you, Blake. I appreciate it. The dream was mine, but I can't take full credit." His head shifted to look around the room. "This is Aria's vision. She's the one who conceptualized all of this. I just told her my idea. She's the one that brought it to life." He looked over at me with love and pride.

"If that's true, then you're a talented woman." He winked. "As well as a beauty." He raised his glass to me.

Marisol's smile turned to a smirk upon hearing the accolades. Blake detected her change in demeanor and turned to her. "Don't you agree?"

His challenge meant that all eyes were on her and she quickly turned on her charm. The fraudulent act didn't escape me.

"Yes, Aria. You're quite the talent. You certainly can work a room … probably as well as you work the gentlemen." She brought her drink to her lips.

I understood the veiled reference, but I wasn't like her. I didn't use sex to gain praise. Her audacity did render me speechless for a moment, but Declan was quite skilled at her game.

"You're correct, Marisol." He gave me a lust-filled look. "She's not only a very accomplished businesswoman, but she has me wrapped around her finger."

I blushed at his obscene and devilish tone. He narrowed his eyes and gave Marisol a scathing look. Anyone else would have been afraid of the animosity in his eyes.

Blake intervened to keep the peace. "I do believe you've made this beautiful woman blush."

Marisol shot both men a contemptuous look as they laughed at her expense. She stomped away in a huff.

Declan shrugged. "Do you think it was something I said?"

As they laughed again, I tried to hide a smile.

To say the evening was overwhelming would have been an understatement. I was introduced to more people than I had known my entire life. I had even more respect for Declan after seeing the way that his peers regarded him.

He was perfection in his Dolce & Gabbana tuxedo. The midnight blue shade complemented my gown perfectly. I felt beautiful in my dress and Declan was the epitome of the perfect man. I caught myself staring at him several times. It was hard to believe he was mine.

The downside to being so dressed up was that it wasn't comfortable for me—specifically, for my feet. Because Declan was mingling with so many people, we barely sat down. I felt a little overwhelmed and anxious, so I took a moment to slip away to the ladies' room. I needed a moment to take a deep breath, touch up my make-up, and get a second wind.

I was checking my reflection in the mirror while I smoothed the top of my hair. I felt an eerie chill on the back of my neck and I knew it was Marisol.

"Honestly. You don't think that will help, do you?"

Marisol had moved into attack position at the mirror next to mine. I refused to give her the satisfaction of acknowledging her presence, but she moved slightly as she baited me.

"Seriously, Aria, you should take a good look at yourself." She made a motion with her finger that went up and down my frame. "Then go out and look at Declan. Even *you* can see that he has no business with the likes of *you*. You may have been his employee for this project, but that's where it will end. Face it. You've outlived your usefulness."

I saw everything in the mirror; her smug face, condescending actions, and air of superiority. Anger filled me; still, I held my composure and ignored her. She wanted a reaction. It wasn't until she moved her face right next to mine that I started to lose control.

"Of course, since you were sleeping with him the entire time, I assume you were paid for other services as well."

Everything felt as if it was moving in slow motion. I didn't recognize the rage that erupted inside of me. I turned and made eye contact with her. We were so close, I could feel her breath. I lifted my clutch and tucked it under my arm. Marisol held her stance. She looked confident, her cocky posture and egotistical smile speaking volumes. She was certain that her goal had been met.

I spoke slowly and succinctly. Enunciating every word, I spat them in her face. "You, of all people, are an expert in that area. I'm sure the room is filled with men who've sampled *your* talents."

It took a minute for the slur to register. Her face contorted with vicious rage. "You bitch!"

She raised her hand to slap me. I was grateful for the advantage of doing manual labor. I wasn't afraid to break a nail to protect myself. I caught her skinny wrist in mid-air and pushed her back against the counter. She struggled, but I didn't let go. I used the leverage to pen her against the counter. One of my curls came loose and fell in my face, but I held my chin high. I spoke through gritted teeth.

"Stay away from me. And stay away from Declan. I know our paths will cross, but don't *ever* make the mistake of attacking me again. Tonight, I'm letting you walk out of here. Next time, you won't be so lucky."

I backed up and flung her away from me. As I straightened, she stumbled. My hand was on the door handle. I was done with her bullshit, but she had to get in the last word.

"This is your *only* warning, Aria."

What the hell was that supposed to mean? I didn't turn around. "Is that a threat or a promise?"

I walked out, not waiting for a reply. I headed toward the nearest exit to get some air. My chest hurt. My ears were ringing. I was shaking on the inside and my hands and knees were unsteady. Aimee noticed and followed me outside.

"What happened?

"I'm fine."

"That's not an answer." Her voice was full of concern. "Let me guess. Marisol?"

My eyes began to fill with tears of frustration and a queasy feeling fed my stomach. She put her hand on my arm in a comforting gesture.

"Not tonight, Aria. Don't let her get to you. This is as much your night as it is Declan's."

My voice choked with the strain of unshed tears. "She's disturbed. I mean really crazy."

"True, but don't let her ruin this for you. That's what she wants." She reached up and tucked the curl back into place. "Besides, I might have to go after a bitch if you ruin your make-up."

A nervous laugh erupted and Aimee smiled. It only took her a minute to fix my hair and dab at my face. "There you go. Now you're perfect."

After a few deep breaths, I regained my composure. I didn't hear Declan approach.

"Beautiful, happy women. That's what I like to see."

As he came closer, he detected my unease. "What's wrong?"

"I'm good," I said, putting my hand in his.

He frowned and drew me closer. "Details. Now or later."

Aimee backed away, leaving us alone. My gaze lowered to the ground and I bit the inside of my cheek to hold my emotions in check. "Later." I took another lungful of air and stood up straight. I could get through this. If not for myself, then for him. I refused to let Marisol ruin our night.

I looked into his eyes and placed my hand on his cheek. "Right now, I want to share this night with you."

He nodded and then lowered his mouth to mine. His kiss filled me with determination. He took my hand. Before he opened the door, he kissed the side of my head and spoke in a low tone. "Later."

CHAPTER
Forty-Seven

Declan

L ife was good. The Studio had been open for well over a month. Katherine informed me that space was booked solid for the next two months. With Aimee's assistance, I advertised for potential models and we had a pool of prospects to interview in two categories: runway and catalogue. Work consumed Aimee and me because we were still under contract with Bella Matrix. I had negotiated more personal control in my last contract, which allowed me more time for both Aria and The Studio.

It took a few days, but Aria finally related what had occurred the night of the opening. I was pissed. I wanted to confront Marisol, but Aria convinced me that it was better to not react at all. She was afraid that if I alienated Marisol, it could jeopardize my relationships with some key clients that I was trying to bring on board. I agreed to play nice with Marisol for the sake of business. Because of my contract, I was obligated to pair with her for a few clients on location shoots. I was hoping to eventually funnel most of my work through The Studio. All of this was going through my head as I lay in bed beside Aria.

"I feel something warm." Her sleepy voice interrupted my

thoughts.

"Don't you mean *someone*?"

"*Someone ... something* ... It's all a blur when your eyes haven't opened."

"Maybe I should help you make the distinction." I brushed the dangling hair away from her neck and kissed at the curve.

"Nope. Still can't tell." Her words were playfully spoken in a singsong manner.

"No?" I baited her, lightly running my hand up and down her bare shoulder and down to her ribcage. I flipped her over and was rewarded with a huge laugh. The corners of her eyes crinkled with delight. *My God*, I would never tire of seeing her face in the morning. I held her wrist with one hand and tickled her side with the other. "Does this refresh your memory?"

She laughed as she made an effort to catch her breath. "Yes! I remember, *I remember*!" She tried in vain to push my fingers away from her ribs, but lifted her head and pecked me on the cheek. "You're my Bear."

"Yes, I am." I growled into her neck. "Don't you ever forget it."

After a gratifying morning shower with her, I went into the kitchen. I had promised her hot coffee and pancakes from scratch. She followed behind me in bare feet and one of my tee shirts. As she was reaching into the cabinet for our cups, there was a knock on the door. We gave each other a surprised look as she placed the cups on the counter.

"Are we expecting anyone?"

"Not that I'm aware of."

I went to the door and returned with a plant almost as tall as me. Her eyes widened.

"What did we do to earn that jolly green giant?"

"Apparently another gift for The Studio."

She pulled the envelope from the plant and opened the card. "It doesn't say it's from anyone specific. It just says *Good luck with your new business.*"

"God knows there are enough plants at The Studio. We can keep this one here."

"Okay. It would look nice in the living room." She pointed to an empty spot. "Right over there. The sunlight's perfect. Not too much."

"Whatever you think, babe. I don't know a damn thing about plants."

She rolled the bulky pot to the designated place.

My tasty breakfast, now brunch, was done. I carried the pancake-laden plates to the table. Weekends were my favorite time. Our work kept us busy and we'd been together for so long that our routines were fairly predictable. I got to spend uninterrupted time with her on the weekends and I couldn't imagine not having her around.

While she was talking, I zoned out. I used to look at my brother and Lacey and never understood that feeling that made you lonely without the other person. Loving Aria showed me how selfish and narcissistic I used to be. I'm still selfish, but only about my time with her. Loving her had become my priority.

"What do you think, Bear?"

Shit! "What? I'm sorry."

"Really?" She cocked her head, snickering. "Did you hear *anything* I said?"

"Um, no …" I hung my head to hide my smile.

"You're a *mess*, you know that?" She pointed her fork at me. "But you make great pancakes."

CHAPTER
Forty-Eight

Marisol

Marisol sat in a rental car making minor adjustments to the listening device that she had purchased from the electronics store. If one bug was good, two were better. The salesman had assured her that she would have sound clarity from a few hundred feet.

She was losing patience with the private investigator; he kept giving her boring reports. She needed to hear about how Declan interacted with Aria, not what restaurant they frequented. Now she could keep tabs on Aria when she came and went from the house. The other information was useless.

As for this little device, it functioned quite well. She could hear Declan and Aria clearly, though nothing they were saying was of much importance. Since she already knew Declan's work schedule for New York, the listening device would let her know when he was going to his little studio. Today was just for practice. She was pleased with what she had heard so far.

Her plan was to make herself a more frequent visitor to The Studio. She was, after all, one of the best. Declan's little wannabes would be star struck. She had a plan to bring him back to his senses.

His judgment had been clouded since he met Aria and if she executed her plan well, Declan would soon be back in the real world.

Just the thought of that plain bitch made her jaw clench with resentment. As her hands tightened on the steering wheel, thoughts of revenge flooded her mind. She would make him pay for the embarrassment that he caused her. Clients were beginning to whisper and talk about why they weren't together. That could not be tolerated. She would win him back and then make him grovel and beg for her forgiveness; but it was the thought of exacting revenge on Aria that gave her the most pleasure. She felt a smile lift the corners of her mouth. An almost sensual, physical pleasure flowed as she mentally exacted revenge on that ugly girl. She'd thought of her over a hundred times. With each instance, a different means of disposing of her came together. The sordid, pleasurable thoughts were becoming more and more frequent. Would she make her suffer by taking Declan away from her? Maybe she would corner *her* in a bathroom and slowly slice her, marring whatever attraction it was that Declan found appealing. Of course it would be done so that she'd be repulsive to Declan and to any other man who'd be *stupid* enough to want her. Other body parts could also be rendered useless. *Oh, yes.* Whatever she decided would be painful for them both. He and the puta deserved to be hurt in a way that was memorable.

Her scheming thoughts brought a pleasure and contentment that she hadn't felt in quite some time. She relaxed against the leather seats, confident that the perfect opportunity would present itself for a tragic end to the sick fascination Declan had with Aria. Marisol would give the little beach whore *exactly* what was coming to her. One thing was for certain; it *wouldn't* be Declan.

Her musings created a stirring deep inside that was sexually hot, but affectionately cold. Affection was a gift that she had never given anyone. She'd take Declan's body and once he'd had a taste of *her,* he'd *never* want another woman. All men felt that way. It was her talent. It was her purpose. She took what she wanted from men before they could take what they wanted from her. She would remind

Declan of how lucky he was. *She* was the beautiful woman in all of the ads with him. *She* was the woman who brought out the sexuality that Declan displayed in the photographs. No man could fake what she saw in those pictures. He wanted her. She would help him find his way back to her and to the pleasures that only she could bring him. She'd get him back to New York. He didn't belong here in this sand town. All it would take was one night with her. He just needed to feel her body, hot and close to him, and his memory would take over. He would be grateful to have her ... to take her ... as all men wanted ... *as all men did.*

She ran her tongue over her lips. *Yes*! The mental images made her writhe and squirm in her seat. She brought her hand down and slipped her fingers between her thighs. The thought of having him naked and at at her mercy was deliciously satisfying. She would take him and her body would control him. All of him. His money, his sex, his mind, and his business.

CHAPTER
Forty-Nine

Aria

I was looking through some real estate listings when Paige arrived. She took a seat as the hostess handed us menus.

"Have a nice dinner, ladies."

"We will," we both said in unison.

I laid the menu down on the table. "Hey, girl! It's so good to see you. I've missed you!"

We hadn't seen each other since the opening of The Studio. I'd been busy with my own business and life with Declan kept me happily occupied. Paige had been busy with her business as well. This was the first time we'd been able to coordinate our schedules.

"I've missed you, too! It's been ages!"

The waiter came over and took our drink order. Once he left, I turned my attention back to my friend.

"So, what's new in your world?"

"Not much." She flipped her hair over her shoulder. "Same old, same old. Dating a little and working a lot. What about you?"

"Always busy, it seems. I'm up and down Coastal Highway constantly with renovations. When Declan isn't at The Studio he's away. What little time he spends at home, I like to spend with him."

"How is everything going with The Studio? Is he happy with it?"

The subject brought a smile to my face. "Everything looks promising. He's focused and determined. He and Aimee have been meeting with prospective models and studio space is booked for months."

"It sounds as if it's going better than you expected."

I leaned back in my chair. "I'm not exactly sure what I expected, to tell the truth," I confided. "Declan was concerned that there would be this big rush of activity in the beginning and then the novelty would wear off. He's become almost fixated on doing whatever it takes to make the business work. He won't turn down any opportunity for new business. And he's become more money-minded. I get the impression that he may have signed a few people when he didn't want to, just for the commission. I'm not sure that I like the idea that he might be compromising himself. On the other hand, he knows his industry. I have to trust him." I tried to shake my uneasy feeling and took a sip of my drink. "Anyway, he and Aimee are always coming and going. They have their own modeling work, as well as the studio business."

Paige moved her glass after taking a sip and gave me a serious look. "Is that a good thing? What about you? Are you happy?"

"I *am* happy. I'm content. Peaceful. Being with Declan is the best thing that's happened to me. I mean, we have our ups and downs like everyone else. When I look back, I think the biggest thing that's come out of our relationship is that I see myself differently."

Paige was eating a piece of bread and butter, but stopped chewing to give me a concerned look. "I don't like the way you're saying that. It makes you sound like you were nothing before him and that's not true. I've known you forever. You've always been great. You don't need to be different."

"If I were on the outside looking in, I'd never picture someone like Declan being with someone like me."

"Oh my god! Aria …"

"No, let me finish." I interrupted because I knew what she was going to say. I needed to make my argument. "He spends a lot of time with models. They're all gorgeous and I'm not. You can't tell me you don't have some insecurities. Sometimes, when I look in the mirror, all I see are flaws. Don't you have days like that?"

She nodded. "I do."

"Then don't we all fall victim? Almost every woman I know does. I didn't think like this before I was around all these women. I take mental inventory when I look in the mirror of what I'd like to fix. It could be something as simple as needing to lose a few pounds or something as serious as contemplating plastic surgery."

A defensive look crossed her face. "You know that I've had plastic surgery. Are you judging me?"

"No, no … not at all. You had plastic surgery for the right reasons and you aren't trying to meet someone else's expectation of what you should look like. And I'm not opposed to women working on themselves. It can be a good thing. I think women should do whatever they have to, to feel confident in themselves, but not to make someone else happy."

She nodded. "I agree with you, but I always thought you were happy with yourself. You seem so confident. Even when we were younger. I always thought you were so sweet and pretty."

"I think I'm as good as any other everyday woman. We act. We let others see what we want them to see. Sweet, pretty, and confident. Secretly, I think we all live a lie. Every time we look in the mirror we tear ourselves to shreds. I wish that I could look at myself the way that Declan looks at me."

She smiled and shook her head. "Do you realize that you smile every time you say his name?"

Her statement warmed me inside. "He *does* make me smile. And as far as how pretty someone is? He always points out the differences between manufactured and true beauty."

"It makes me sad to think of you as insecure. I've always

thought you were beautiful."

"Yeah. I only wish I saw myself like that. My thighs are dimpled and my hair is too curly, but I'm learning to love my features. It's just hard when I compare myself to the women I see at The Studio. That's what the world wants. I wonder if, someday, it will be what Declan wants again."

Paige was quiet for a few minutes as she mulled over my thoughts.

"Okay. Let me put it this way. Did you love your dad?"

A wave of shock crashed over me. "What? Of course I did!"

"Yeah, well, he lost himself piece by piece, but you and your mom still loved him. He might have thought less of himself, but neither of you did. The disease didn't make you love him any less. If anything, you loved him more for his bravery. Declan is handsome, which I'm sure can be a real pain to his girlfriend, but it doesn't make you love him any less. And I know you. If he weren't a good man on the inside, it wouldn't matter to you how he looks. He thinks you're beautiful. You have to cut that insecure cancer out, or your insecurities could ruin a good thing."

"He really is good, isn't he?"

"*You're* good ..."

"I know."

We sat quietly for a few minutes, letting the conversation sink in. Paige reached across the table and put her hand over mine.

"He's lucky to have you, you know that?"

I started laughing. "Stop. You're going to make me cry."

"I don't care. He's lucky to have you. You've taught him that love changes everything."

CHAPTER
Fifty

Aria

It had been a good visit. The conversation made me feel better. More confident. It had been a long day, but I decided to drive by The Studio to see Declan. He was working late, but my talk with Paige had made me miss him. I wanted to see him, even if just for a few moments.

He had mentioned that Blake Matthews was sending down a small group of prospects. They were young, hopeful, and nervous. Blake thought that Declan could serve as a mentor to them and let them know what to expect when venturing into the industry. Hearing the benefits and pitfalls from someone who was respected would give them a realistic view. I couldn't think of a more qualified person than Declan.

"Hi, Aria!" Katherine called out to me as I strolled into the lobby. "How have you been?"

I couldn't help but smile. "Great! How are you, Katherine? I haven't seen you in a while."

"I can't complain. Declan's still in a meeting

"I don't want to bother him. If you think he'll be long, I'll just meet him at home."

Katherine rolled her eyes. "He would never think that and you know it. He should be almost finished. He's in the large conference room. You can go around and take a peek."

"Thanks. We'll get together soon, okay?"

"Absolutely! Just let me know when and I'll be there."

I rounded the corner to go to the bay side of the building. The sun was beginning to set as dusk approached. We had chosen that location for the conference room to make a powerful impact. The view of the bay was unobstructed and beautiful.

I saw him sitting at the head of the dark mahogany table. The group was small and very attractive, but I couldn't tear my eyes away from him. He was so handsome and confident. He carried himself so well. What teenager wouldn't want to be like him? He was a perfect example of what they should aspire to be and was a credit to the fashion industry. Although I couldn't hear his words, I could see that he spoke with passion. I could also tell that whatever the topic was, it brought him pleasure. He wore a smile that made my heart clench. There was no way his enthusiasm wasn't infectious.

No one else at the table looked to be over the age of twenty-one. Three gorgeous girls and two handsome young men were all focused on Declan. They each had a folder in front of them. I recognized it. Aimee, Katherine, Declan, and I had sat at that same table, assembling those packets.

Declan was the originator of much of the information. He dictated relevant information as Katherine took notes. Brochures were made and laid out on the table. A few pizzas and a couple of beers later, and we'd put them all together. *Now look at him.*

I saw someone move at the back of the room. As I followed the group's line of sight, I saw her. Adrenaline made my nervous system hit overdrive. Marisol.

The sight caught me off guard. She spoke to the small group, then stopped and smiled at Declan.

As each of the models exited the room, they approached him. I stood across the hall and watched everything unfold like I was watching a movie. Marisol was the villainess.

"Thank you, Mr. Sinclair. That was great. I know so much more now."

"My pleasure. I hope the information I provided will help. You need the proper tools in order to make a good decision. Read it over and please feel free to call with any questions."

It felt like I watched forever and all I could think about was *Marisol, Marisol, Marisol.* I thought my brain was going to explode because there was no reason why she should be here. Finally, after the last person left, he came over to me.

"Hey beautiful. This is a nice surprise. I didn't know you were stopping by." He bent down to kiss me, but I moved my head. "I wouldn't have if I'd known you had company. What the hell is she doing here?" I nodded toward the room at the exact moment that Marisol walked through the door. She could tell by the look on my face that I was upset and she reveled in it.

"Hello, Aria. So nice to see you."

Her sugary fake voice only pissed me off more. "Marisol." I barely acknowledged her and acid dripped in my tone. She ignored me and went over to Declan. I nearly ripped her hand off when she placed it on his shoulder.

"Those kids hung on every word you said. You were great!"

He smiled at the compliment and seemed to enjoy her accolades. "Thanks. I like helping them. I'm sure they had it figured out before they came here."

"Oh, you're being modest! Why don't you let me get them to-gether and take them back to New York in the limo. It will really give them a taste of the good life. You remember how the high life is, don't you?"

"Wonderful," I muttered under my breath. It must have been a little louder than I thought because they both turned. He frowned. She sneered.

"*Ciao, guapo.*" She bussed his cheek with an air kiss. Turning toward me, she wrinkled her nose like she smelled something bad. "*Ciao*, Aria." Making a grand exit, she swayed her ass so much as she went toward the group of young people that I thought she might throw out a hip. I turned to Declan, the loathing for her rising up within me. My impulse was to interrogate. "What the hell was that?"

He was clueless. "What was *what?*"

"Marisol! When did *she* become a Studio *regular?*"

"Blake sent her down with the kids. It was business. That's all."

"It doesn't look like Marisol thinks that's all there is to it. You need to open your eyes, Declan. You may think it was innocent enough, but she's more cunning than that."

"It doesn't matter what she thinks, Aria." His voice boomed authoritatively, his stance firm. "This is *my* business and *I* said that's all it is."

Marisol was playing her game and she wasn't even here. She'd inserted herself between us, her presence invisibly thick and manipulative. Was this the kind of crap she pulled when they were working together? Some sort of reverse passive/aggressive head game? Could he really be that blind? Did it only take batting eyelashes and a wiggling ass to get him to roll over and play dead? She was a threat to his business and to us. She pulled this crap every time she was near me. He had seen it before. Why not now?

"Since when did you become so comfortable with her? You used to *hate* when she was anywhere near us. So what is it? Is it about her influence? Is it about the money she can bring to The Studio?"

He scoffed.

"That's it, isn't it? Blake sends her down here and all of a sudden, you feel validated. Money and Marisol. Is that what this is about?"

He shot me a cold glare.

"You can't fool me, Dec, I know you too well. She looked at you like you were a piece of prime meat and she looked at me like I was a piece of shit."

"Aria, knock it off. You're overreacting. I can handle her."

I was angry and upset. "I don't think I am. And I don't think you can." I knew I was right; I could feel it.

"Well, I do." He was dismissive. "All she was doing was sitting in the back of a room."

I opened my mouth to object, but he wouldn't let me.

"Aria! End of story."

CHAPTER
Fifty-One

Aria

Who the hell does he think he is? "It's not the 'end of story!' It's just the beginning for her. Her grand exit? The flattery? Kissing you on the cheek? All of that was for my benefit!"

We were at a stand-off. Our points of view were miles apart. He crossed his arms; his shoulders were stiff and his legs were braced far apart, like he was facing an enemy. He was ready for a fight. So was I. I wasn't backing down.

"Not everything is directed at you, Aria. Don't be so paranoid. That's the way she says goodbye to everyone, not just me. And yes, I'm glad Blake sent her down. Do you know how flattered those kids were? The two most successful people in this industry were in the same room with them. It's not a big deal."

Was he really that blind? "It's a big deal to me. A *very* big deal. She's trying to hurt *us*. You're not seeing it and I think it's all because you want the business to succeed so badly that all you can think of is the almighty dollar!"

"Aria! Stop it! You're letting your insecurities get the best of you!" He turned his back to me.

I wasn't done with this. "Screw you! I can't believe you would throw that up to me. Something I told you in confidence and you're using it against me? Because of Marisol? That's a low blow. She's a bitch. *She* doesn't make me insecure. The fact that she's a psycho and a stalker is what's on the table here. Maybe you should get the dollar signs out of your eyes. You can't see how unstable she is. She'll use any excuse to get close to you and right now you might just be money-hungry enough to let her!"

He turned out the lights in the conference room, grabbed my hand, and led me through the door.

"I don't want to talk about this anymore. We're going home."

I yanked my hand from his. "I don't want to go home."

We stared at each other for several moments, our chests heaving, our nostrils flaring. Neither of us were giving in. Declan looked up at the ceiling and took a deep breath. He was on one side of the corridor; I was on the other.

"Aria, look. I'm going to have to be around her. If The Studio is going to thrive and grow she's going to be here once in a while. I might not like her, but her name lends a lot of credibility. You have to understand business to realize that sometimes it's a game."

"Really, Declan?" My smartass tone responded to his condescending one. "Talking down to me, when I helped you? Don't use your business to justify having Marisol around. You're compromising us for her and you're justifying it with business. Think about what you're doing, because it matters. On so many levels."

"It doesn't matter and it isn't about you. But it is about business. *My business.* Not everything is personal and if you wouldn't have just dropped in like that ..."

He stopped dead.

Everything became clear.

"So ... what? What would have happened? You would have whisked her out the door? Or you would have told me not to come?" I waited for an answer. He just glared at me. Anger filled me until I was livid. I threw my purse over my shoulder. "That's what I thought."

Tears threatened to spill as I turned and walked away from him. I heard him call my name, but I just kept walking. I was angry and hurt. He couldn't see it. He *wouldn't* see it. She was playing puppeteer and using all of the men in her world to get what she wanted. Declan. Blake. Her games and tactics pissed me off. If I stayed any longer, I would say things that I'd later regret. The better decision was to walk away.

I couldn't go to his house and I didn't want to go to mine because I thought he might follow me there. Paige's house wasn't far. I called to tell her that I was coming. I needed some space. Marisol. I could call her many things. Bitch, conniver, manipulator, liar, parasite, elitist, deviant, leech, psychopath—the list was endless. She was a chameleon. She had a way of twisting things to make it look like she was doing you a favor. It terrified me. Something was going on. She had an agenda; I could feel it. She wouldn't waste the energy unless there was a benefit for her. I didn't know what her ulterior motive was, but I was going to find out. Then her true incentive would be exposed. Declan had been ready to lie to me because of her. It didn't matter if it was a lie of omission or not. He would never have told me that she was in Ocean City. She was infiltrating our lives with her evil. Marisol had to be stopped.

CHAPTER
Fifty-Two

Aria

Things had changed in just a few hours. I had gone from praising him at dinner to cursing him over a bottle of wine. And Paige had to hear all of it. I felt like a fool. Thankfully, she had a good supply of Kleenex.

My phone was blowing up from Declan's calls. At first, I let it go to voicemail. It wasn't just that I was pissed-off at him; I also didn't trust what would come out of my mouth. I was that angry. After the ninth call, I answered, but I didn't give him a chance to speak. Once we were connected, I said, "I'm fine. I'm at Paige's. I'll see you tomorrow." *Click.* Then I threw my phone in my bag while Paige refilled my glass.

At first I was so upset that I didn't say anything. Then everything came pouring out—the anger, the hurt, and the doubt. I questioned myself, him, and the situation. She listened. At the end of my rant, I waited for her to say something.

"What? Tell me. Do you think I overreacted?"

Her brows furrowed as she cocked her head to the side. "I don't know if you really want my opinion or if you just want me to agree with you."

"By the look on your face, I can almost tell what you're thinking. You think I'm crazy. But I see through her. Just because I don't have any proof, doesn't mean that it isn't happening."

"I do understand, sweetie. I remember Aimee telling me that this woman was bad news, but just because she was there doesn't mean something's going on. She was in a public place with a lot of people around. It's probably just business."

"Seriously. When have you ever known me to be an alarmist?" I felt defeated that she wasn't siding with me, but she wasn't disputing me either. "Yeah. That's what I thought." I held out my glass and she poured some more. I took a few gulps, enjoying the calming effect of the wine. "Think back to when I first told you about her. Do you remember? She acted like he was property that I took from her."

Paige nodded.

"It never gets any better. Every time, she baits me. At every opportunity. Even though he assures me that there was never anything between them, she acts like I am the intruder. No … let me correct that—she attacks me—verbally and there has even been some physical contact."

Her eyes widened. "How much of this have you told Declan?

Overwhelming emotions hit me at the same time, causing my eyes to glaze with tears. "I've told him everything. The only thing I left out, until tonight, was telling him that I think there's something seriously wrong with her. Something more than jealousy. She is obsessed with him."

I pulled my knees to my chest. Paige reached out and patted me. "Don't let her get to you."

"I can't help it. My dad always told me to go with my gut. Right now, my gut's telling me that Marisol is bat-shit crazy. I'm so tired of these mind games. It's the same thing over and over. It just drones in my head, especially when I know I'm going to be around her. I just feel so paranoid. I think Aimee's the only one who sees that she's jealous, but I think it's *more* than that. Today, when I saw her, I lost it. I *never* behave that way. I don't like her and I sure as hell don't like how I got because of her. And the fact that he wasn't taking me seriously? That hurt, Paige."

She moved next to me and I laid my head on her shoulder.

"Try talking to him again. Tell him exactly what you've told me. If he loves you like I think he does, he'll know you reacted more out of love than jealousy."

I shook my head and looked away. "My gut's telling me something else. I don't know what it is, but there are warning bells going off. I don't know if he'll listen."

It was three in the morning. I settled into Paige's guest room, the bed easing my physical ache. As I slipped under the covers, I pulled out my phone. There was one message.

Declan: *I miss you. We need to talk and we will. I didn't want you to go to sleep without knowing that I love you. I was overtired. Come home in the morning. We'll talk. Over coffee :)*

I smiled. I loved the life we'd created, but I didn't want to be dragged into his old one.

Paige walked me to my car and gave me a hug.

"Thanks for listening. I really appreciate it."

"No problem. What are friends for?" Concern shadowed her features. "I know he'll be stubborn. He's going to rationalize that he can divide Marisol into two categories: personal and professional. And maybe he can, but you have to be on your guard." She held me by the shoulders, her expression serious. "I also know you. If you *truly* feel there's a reason for concern, then make him see it."

I gave her another hug. "Thanks for putting up with me."

"Not a problem." She closed my car door, smiled, and winked. "Now, go straighten out that man of yours!"

I drove down Coastal Highway. I didn't turn on the radio. I needed the white noise of the droning hum of the road. I thought of my encounters with Marisol. I couldn't control her, but I could control me. It was amazing what a few hours of sleep and a bit of distance could do for your perspective. The challenge was figuring out how to convince Declan that he needed to be on guard for the chaos that Marisol was capable of.

I pulled up to the back of his house and took three deep breaths. Declan and I had never fought like this before. Last night had been unbearable for me and as I walked up the steps, I hoped he felt the same way.

I opened the door and let myself in. It was really early. I went toward the kitchen to make some coffee, hoping for a little more time to think through what I was going to say. I rounded the corner and stopped. Declan was sitting at the table. His hair was disheveled, his face had stubble, and his eyes were tired and red. I felt the tears as they welled up in my eyes. I dropped my purse and jacket by the sink and felt him watching me.

"I made coffee." His voice was soft, but rough.

"Thanks, I'll get a cup." I washed and dried my hands, hoping to steady the shaking. Then I poured my coffee and turned around to look at him. I was unsure what to do next. He pushed out a chair with his foot.

"Come sit down."

I did as he asked, holding onto my cup with both hands and looking at the floor. His voice was a soft command.

"Aria, look at me." As I lifted my eyes, he continued. "First, I want to say I missed you ..."

I could feel a lump forming in my throat.

"Second, we have to talk about what happened ..."

Yes, we did have to talk. I removed my lips from the cup and gave him a weak smile. "You look like hell."

His smile mirrored mine. "I feel like hell."

I shrugged. "You can go first."

He looked extremely apprehensive. "Okay. Me first." He leaned forward and put his elbows on the table. "You seemed to be on board. I know I've been busier. My schedule is erratic. My meetings are unpredictable and our plans are changed at the last minute. But I'm just starting out." He ran his hands over his face in an exasperated movement. "I'm doing business with both old contacts and new. I feel like I'm burning the candle at both ends. I just thought that you were behind me."

"Is that what you think this is about?" My forehead creased and my body tensed. "I'm not upset about your business."

"Then what, Aria? I get that you were pissed about Marisol, but once she was gone you were still pissed. I'm tired. I spend a lot of time working crazy hours and I'm not always home. I really don't know what you're mad about." His eyes were pleading as he ran his hands through his hair.

I got up from my seat and went over to him. Sitting in his lap, I wrapped my arms around his neck. He lifted his chin and I looked into his eyes. "It wasn't about the business."

"Then what?"

"I was pissed last night, but I couldn't be more proud of you."

He looked puzzled.

"Then what—"

I interjected before he could ask. "It's Marisol. We need to talk about Marisol."

CHAPTER
Fifty-Three

Declan

Marisol. I listened to everything Aria had to say about her. Although I understood her concern, I didn't want her to be alarmed. She believed Marisol to be a threat and I thought she was a nuisance.

Aria sat on my lap. My arms were wrapped around her waist. "You do realize that we're probably never going to see eye-to-eye about her, don't you, babe?"

"Yes." There was sorrow in her whisper as she rested her head against mine. "That's what bothers me. I have a bad feeling about her."

"I'll keep my guard up."

She placed her delicate hands on the sides of my unshaven face. "Promise? I can't explain how I feel. I just know she's trouble."

"How can I say no to such a beautiful face?" I placed my lips to hers. "Don't run away again. Last night was hell."

"I couldn't help it. I was overwhelmed. I needed to get away. It was better than standing there screaming at you."

"No, it wasn't," I confessed. "I'd rather have you scream at me than run away. Promise you won't do that again."

She locked her arms around my neck and gave me a hug. "I'll try." She grinned impishly.

I smiled back, gripping her around the waist. I stood up and spun her around.

"Stop, you crazy ass! You're making me dizzy!"

"I'm only crazy because of you."

As much as I would have liked to just hang out with Aria the whole day, we were expecting my brother. Carter was still struggling without Lacey and we thought it would be good to invite him to stay with us for a change of scenery. After our talk, Aria said she was going shopping so that she could make a nice dinner. I told her that I'd get the house ready for Carter's arrival. As I heard her car start, I poured the last of the coffee from the pot into my cup.

She'd given me a lot to think about. I chastised myself for letting anything interfere with our relationship. We'd worked too hard to get where we were. She had never let her business interfere with our personal life, so I had to find a way to do the same. The problem was finding a way to interact with Marisol that wouldn't impact my personal life.

I wasn't blind. Marisol was manipulative, but she was more an inconvenience than a threat. Aria didn't know her as well as I did. I could handle Marisol. I'd done it for years. This was the same catty bullshit that she pulled all the time. I had to occasionally tolerate her presence at The Studio, but I needed a better plan. I had to be able to work with Marisol and assure Aria that I wouldn't let her come between us. If I could make Aria feel more secure, Marisol would just be an afterthought.

A knock interrupted my thoughts. *Carter! Idiot must have forgotten his key.* I went to the door with a huge smile and swung it open.

"What the hell, Carter! You forget how to get in my …"

"I see you weren't expecting me, but I'll let myself in." Marisol brushed by my chest and went into the living room. I slammed the door.

"What do *you* want? I thought you went back to New York."

"Oh Declan, I'm hurt. You aren't happy to see me?" She pulled an envelope from her handbag. "I have some papers for you to look at. Blake wanted me to give them to you. It's in regard to the group he sent to The Studio."

"Why didn't you give this to me last night? I took the envelope from her hand, grabbed a pen, and signed. I didn't even look at it.

She came closer to me. "Well, that would be my professional ethics." Resting her hand on my arm, she pushed her pelvis against me. Lifting just her eyes, she gave me a sultry look. Her intent was clear. "You know I would always go above and beyond for you. You know, to deliver my *best* work."

I moved away. "What are you doing? Don't play the *bitch in heat* game with me. I'm not interested." I shook the envelope in front of her face. "It's signed. Now go."

She moved toward me again. "It really is about work! If you don't believe me, call Blake."

"I signed it. Now get the hell out of my house. The next time you have business to discuss with me, send it to The Studio. Don't come here again."

I shoved the envelope into her hand. She threw herself against me, backing me up to the fireplace. She managed to place her hand on my cheek.

"I don't know what your problem is. Last night, you were back to your old self. Laughing, smiling … I thought we were friends again. Wouldn't you like that? For us to be … *friends*?

She quickly moved her hand and grabbed my crotch. Hard. My brain went into overdrive. Aria was right. She was delusional. I had to get her out of here. But right now, she literally had me by the balls. I needed to talk her down and get rid of her.

"Is that what you want, Marisol? For us to be friends?"

She didn't release her grip. Instead, she gave me a skeptical look. She moved her hip and her lower body pressed into mine. She gradually loosened her fingers.

"I could make you want me."

My jeans were loose and slung low. I hadn't bothered to snap the top button. In one quick move, Marisol shoved her hand inside the waistband. I bolted upright to push her away, but my attention was diverted by the sound of something hitting the floor.

Fragments of a broken starfish scattered as they slid on the wooden floor. Aria's eyes connected with mine as she looked from me to Marisol. As her gaze traveled lower, I watched the breath leave her body. Her arms went around her midsection. She looked like she was going to be sick. It was only for seconds, but it seemed like our eyes locked forever. Too many things showed on her face: shock, anger, and devastating hurt. The scene was horribly wrong.

Everything froze for Aria and me. The devastation in her face ripped my heart out. Marisol took advantage of the moment.

"We didn't expect you so soon ..."

It was an emotional sucker punch. Aria ran out the door.

I exploded, pushing Marisol so hard that she stumbled. "You bitch!"

Her smile was wicked. "It was only a matter of time ..."

I burst through the door and looked in all directions. I had to find Aria. She was down the street, far enough ahead of me that I had to yell for her at the top of my lungs. She wouldn't stop. I chased her. She was so fast! I had to get to her, to explain that she was right and I was wrong.

Desperation burned my lungs as I sucked in air. I couldn't think about the pain in my chest because all I saw was the pain in her face.

"Aria!"

CHAPTER
Fifty-Four

Aria

I ran. Only one image burned in my brain.

Declan.

Marisol.

Declan and Marisol.

Declan and Marisol!!!

With each pounding step, I tried to erase the scene from my mind. I had questions that I didn't want answered. When? Why? How long? *Oh God! Please make it stop! I can't breathe ...*

"Aria!"

I heard his voice, yet I still ran. The tears were flowing as quickly as the adrenaline flooded through me.

"Aria! Stop!"

I don't want to talk to him. Yes, I do! I don't want to see him. Yes, I do! I want my heart to stop beating so hard. It's breaking! I don't want him near me. I want him to hold me!

Everything was a complete jumble. I didn't have a single rational thought. I just wanted to keep running. *But where will I go?* I ran toward the bay side.

"Aria! Stop! Please!"

Something about his tone made me stop. I didn't know what it was. Maybe I recognized a kindred terror. Slowing down, I bent over and placed my hands on my thighs, I struggled for breath. I didn't know where I was, as if I were in a daze. My arms and legs wouldn't move.

I tried to focus. I was on Coastal Highway at the edge of the curb. Traffic whizzed by me. Declan's shouting alerted me to the danger. I looked left and right on the street, across the highway, and at the sides of the buildings. I heard him, but couldn't see him. *Where is he?*

I became distracted, stepping out into the street to gain a better view. Then I saw him. He was on the other side of the highway. His eyes locked with mine and he ran faster. I took a step. My thoughts were completely irrational at this point. Nothing made sense except that I needed to be close to him. My foot hit the blacktop. I was trying to make my way to him and he was coming for me when I saw him look at the oncoming traffic. His voice was filled with a tone of excruciating torment. It rattled me toward clarity as I saw his expression register a look of horror.

"ARIA!!!"

He screamed as I heard screeches of grinding machinery.

"Declan! Go!"

I screamed, but it came out as a whisper. All I could focus on was Declan … and Marisol.

CHAPTER
Fifty-Five

Declan

The sirens sang a shrill and haunting song. An overwhelmed, distraught gentleman held his hand to his chest.

"Oh, my God! Oh, my God! I'm so sorry. I couldn't stop."

Someone was shouting to call nine-one-one. A man dropped to the ground, desperately attempting to administer CPR. The paramedics arrived, bellowing into the increasing crowd. "Move back! We need some room!"

Medical equipment was affixed around the top of an arm. Air was pumped by a ball. A cold stethoscope listened intently for vital information. A light was shined into eyes. Two paramedics exchanged looks. One nodded. There was a pulse. There was still some hope.

We recognized no one, except for each other. Words were unspoken, yet said. Telepathic communication transcended the chaos through a glance. Fear was the ruler of the moment.

My gaze was locked on Aria, willing strength. She poured love into me with her eyes. A touch would have been welcome, but was impossible.

Time was passing quickly; however, for us it dragged out in agony. Every precious moment held a lifetime of regret, love, and hope. All around us, people were taking deliberate emergency medical steps. Intravenous fluids were administered. Stabilization was attempted. Voices carried on the wind.

"I'm going."

"I'm sorry; you can't."

"Try and stop me."

A jolt occurred and a stretcher was loaded into the back of an ambulance. An ear-piercing siren wailed its warning into a heavy stream of cars. Fear was looming. The monster threatened to consume us both.

Brown eyes met blue. Emotions exploded in the colors. One hand was pressed against the other.

"I can't lose you. Stay with me. Please."

***

"There's no way to tell what a person is thinking. Emotional trauma is as much a struggle as physical. They seem to do better when they're together."

As Carter and Jeannie listened to Dr. Dominic's explanation, neither was comforted. "Witnessing an accident can be just as devastating to the mind as physical injuries are to the body. Both of them are struggling, just in different ways. Neither one of them is out of the woods yet."

Concern shrouded Jeannie. The thought of her daughter and Declan in pain was breaking her heart. "But they will recover?"

"I believe so. In time." His words were soft and soothing. Hope pierced the heaviness in the room. "The trauma, when you're helpless, it takes a toll. When they do speak, they ask about each other. That's a good sign."

Jeannie couldn't contain the tears. Carter wrapped his arm around her. How could something like this have happened to Aria and Declan?

"I can tell you that we have hope for them both. People have come back from much worse."

"And what about my brother?" Carter's hand tightened against Jeannie's skin.

"I can't tell you much more. We've done what we can. The rest is up to him."

Jeannie lowered her head. She could no longer control the tears. Her heart broke equally for her daughter and Declan. The couple that seemed so perfect had hit the perfect storm. She could only shake her head in disbelief.

Dr. Dominic took her hand. "I can assure you that they are both receiving the best care."

"Thank you." Her tone was frail. "Anything you can do for them is very much appreciated."

CHAPTER
Fifty-Six

*M*y Aria.

   You look so fragile. I'm afraid you'll break into a million pieces, if I breathe too close. I need you in my arms. I want you in my arms. Where you belong. We're a perfect fit. Ease your mind, baby. Everything's going to be all right. I'm here for you. I love you with all my heart. I want you to know that. I want you to feel my strength. You're my world.

   Please, baby, please …

---

*M*y Declan.

   I can't stand seeing you in pain. I want to make you feel better. When I look at you, it breaks my heart. I watch you sleep. I watch you breathe. All I want is to be near you. I want to curl up against you. I want us to be the way that we were before.

   Please, baby, please …

EPILOGUE

Marisol

T his will do."

Marisol walked slowly over to the desk. The lease only required her signature. It was perfect. A beautiful penthouse condominium with a private garage and elevator and a stunning view of both the ocean and bay. It had been a while since she had played the incognito game and the local residents were just new pawns. She scribbled her name and handed the lease to the agent.

Smiling, he placed the keys in her hand. "Enjoy your stay, Ms. Vencedor. Please call me if you need anything."

The man closed the door quietly behind him as he let himself out. A slow walk around the room made her glow with pride. She could watch the events she had planned unfold with complete anonymity. *Ms. Vencedor.* The alias was clever. There was no doubt that she would be the *winner*.

Declan and Aria made a big mistake when they baited me!

She liked games. She was good at them. Although she had accomplished much in a short time, there was still much to do. Finding a condo with an advantageous viewpoint had been the first step.

It remained to be seen how the fate of the lovebirds would play out and it was best to watch them from the shadows before making her next move. They had underestimated her.

Round two was about to begin.

ABOUT THE
Author

D.D. Lorenzo is a contemporary storyteller who lives in Maryland with her eclectic family. She loves to weave tales about characters that thrill you, break your heart, and leave you begging for more.

Stay connected with D.D.

Facebook:
https://www.facebook.com/ddlorenzo.author

Twitter:
@ddlorenzobooks

Instagram:
https://www.instagram.com/ddlorenzobooks

Website:
www.ddlorenzo.com

Pinterest:
https://www.pinterest.com/ddlorenzo/

Other Titles by D.D. Lorenzo

Imperfection Series

No Perfect Man (Book One)

No Perfect Time (Book Two)

No Perfect Couple (Book Three)

No Perfect Secret (Book Four)

No Perfect Bitch (Book Five)

36468332R00144

Made in the USA
Middletown, DE
16 February 2019